Anonymous

Brief biographies of the members of the Indiana State Government :

executive, judicial, and legislative, 1874-5

Anonymous

Brief biographies of the members of the Indiana State Government : executive, judicial, and legislative, 1874-5

ISBN/EAN: 9783337305550

Printed in Europe, USA, Canada, Australia, Japan

Cover: Foto ©Raphael Reischuk / pixelio.de

More available books at **www.hansebooks.com**

BRIEF BIOGRAPHIES

OF THE

MEMBERS

OF THE

INDIANA STATE GOVERNMENT;

EXECUTIVE, JUDICIAL,

AND LEGISLATIVE.

1874-5.

THE INDIANAPOLIS SENTINEL COMPANY,
PRINTERS AND PUBLISHERS.

INTRODUCTORY.

For the gratification of commendable curiosity on the part of the public, the SENTINEL recently published an eight page supplement containing short sketches of the members of the General Assembly. That enterprise met with such general favor as to warrant the thorough revision of those sketches and their reproduction under cover, together with the members of the Executive and Judicial departments of the State Government of Indiana, outgoing and incoming. The preparation of these sketches for publication was beset with obstacles not easily surmounted. Some most meritorious subjects were sketched but briefly because the necessary data was not accessable. So far as they go, however, all may be regarded as reliable. It has been the purpose of the publishers to be impartial and non-partisan, giving each subject sketched the full benefit of all tho material at hand.|

THOMAS A. HENDRICKS,

GOVERNOR OF THE STATE OF INDIANA.

To write the history of the political and public life of Governor Hendricks would require a book. It should not be attempted here and now, for another reason, viz: That he is yet in the middle of his public career and the proper time has not arrived to comment upon it. A mere outline of the facts on this point may be given as follows: Professionally, a lawyer, and a successful one; he was in the Indiana Legislature from 1845 to 1849, an active member of the Constitutional Convention of 1850 from Shelby county, twice elected to Congress, in 1851 and the succeeding term, in 1855 appointed Commissioner of the General Land Office by President Pierce, which position he held four years, in 1863 chosen to the Senate of the United States, and in 1872, against his wishes, elected Governor of the State of Indiana for the term ending January 13, 1877. Within this condensed summary is contained a political history of great activity, and a brilliance which attracts national attention. There are exciting campaigns, years of service, memorable acts and speeches which together mark the man as one of the foremost living statesmen. As such, he is looked upon in the present and counted on for the future by a people whose confidence and affection, also, he enjoys in the highest degree. Gov. Hendricks is altogether an Indiana citizen. Born, it is true, in Ohio, Muskingum county, September 7, 1819, before the end of his first year his father and mother had come into the Hoosier State, and his first step in life was probably made within the present city of Indianapolis. The family went to Shelby county in 1822 and assaulted nature in her fortresses yet unimproved, It was a rough fight, but healthful to character. The Governor made the most of the common schools, and pursued his studies further in a college of his own State at Hanover, Jeffeason county, which is now proud of her eminent son. Only once he left the State in search of learning, and that was to complete a course of law study with a near relation at Chambersburg, Pennsylvania. This done, he retuned to his life work in his own State. So tenacious is he of utilizing and relying on home resources, that lately in seeking a head officer for the Purdue University, he set his face steadily against going outside of Indiana.

The magnetic charm of Gov. Hendricks lies in his personal character. All men and women and children, too, are attracted to his presence. In his society political prejudice and partisan hostility are inevitably destroyed. They flee away before the genial influence of cordiality, good nature and engaging conversation. Although he always maintains a genteel dignity, the humble,timid, and consciously uncultured, find ease in his society and pleasure at his presence. No man of the people feels restraint in approaching him the second time. He is the life of an excursion party, a reception, or a good time where "two or three are met together." Temperate, sprightly, witty, need it be said that the ladies find in him a companion for travel or the social circle worthy their refined tastes and agreeable at all times. In his disposition, the Governor is by nature conservative. He clings to the old and distrusts the new. Consulting his feelings rather than judgment, he would be inclined to discourage changes and innovations. This comes of nature and is indicative of strong home influences extending back in the family. But they err most egregiously who, not studying him personally, assume that the Governor is non-combative, timid, or vacillating. He is cautious, but if aroused, the impulses of his nature rise to absolute fury. This fact is none the less real, because his strong judgment and will restrain rash demonstrations. It is unnecessary to say that the subject is of handsome face and figure. Most people know that. His manner of speech in private and public is enchanting, and on the political rostrum he is clear, sharp and statesmanlike in style. He is exceedingly happy in short addresses on miscellaneous occasions, having a habit not universally known, of being carefully prepared, when it is supposed the speech is strictly impromptu. One point more must not be omitted in this inadequate sketch. That is the staunch devotion of Gov. Hendricks to the public schools of Indiana. On these he builds all expectations of a worthy citizenship and a prosperous State. Intelligent himself in spite of the adversities of a pioneer history, he demands education for the people and insists upon it everywhere, and at all times. It is not, therefore, unworthy for Indiana to be proud of her own rearing, when her greatest son is known still more widely for his integrity, purity and intrinsic goodness.

LEONIDAS SEXTON,

LIEUTENANT GOVERNOR,

Is a native of Rushville, this State, having been born there May 19th, 1827. His father was born in Massachusetts, his mother in North Carolina, and they moved to Indiana in 1821. Mr. Sexton has lived at Rushville all his life, with the exception of a brief period of time spent at school. · He graduated from Jefferson College, Pennsylvania, in 1846, and then he read law in the office of the Hon. A. W. Hubbard, late member of Congress for three terms, from the sixth Iowa district, but now engaged in banking at Sioux city, in that State. In politics Mr. Sexton was a Whig until the organization of the Republican party. The first vote he ever cast was for President Taylor which was on the second Tuesday of November, 1848. Immediately afterward, on the same day, he took a state room on a palatial boat on the White Water canal, enroute to Cincinnati to attend law lectures by Messrs. Groesbeck and Tilford, the former a prominent politician and eminent jurist, yet living, the latter, then his partner, now deceased. having acquired the necessary legal lore for a beginning, he returned to Rushville and entered upon the practice of his profession, and he has continued to be so engaged ever since then except when in public life. In 1856, he was a candidate for Legislative honors, his opponent being Samuel McBride, Esq. A contest case which lasted all through the session and never was settled, was the result and Rush was not represented in the law-making branch of the government during all that time, yet both contestants drew their pay as regular members. Such cases were then very rare and served to spice the sessions which otherwise might have been monotonous.

In 1872, his friends. without his knowledge and consent in State convention. entered him for the race for the Lieutenant Governorship, and the people. at large. elected him. By virtue of that call and election, he is now the incumbent of that office and as such, President of the Senate. As a lawyer, he has a high standing in his section of the State, and indeed, throughout the State, and has a host of friends at the bar, and among the people. In fact, he possesses all the elements of personal popularity. At home and abroad, he is uniformly kind and generous to the poor. Law students are always anxious to read for the profession in his office. Unlike most members of the bar, he is particularly delighted to assist and advance all worthy young men who show a disposition to help themselves. He never discourages anybody when seeking to step higher upon the ladder of life.

He possesses quick perceptive power, amounting almost to intuition, and at the same time is cool and collected, qualities that peculiarly fit him for wielding the gavel over a deliberative body.

JOHN ENOS NEFF,

SECRETARY OF STATE—INCOMING.

The young and brilliant incumbent of the Secretary of State's office comes down from the tip-top of Indiana. That is to say, he is a native of Winchester, Randolph county, which is the highest land in the State. His parents, the father from Ohio and the mother from Pennsylvania, are Scotch-Irish and German by descent and the family hold a leading position in Randolph county. Mr. Neff's father was the first treasurer of the county, and also a quartermaster with the rank of captain, in the Mexican war. The son is a bright and successful lawyer, having like the State Auditor, laid the foundations of his education at the State University of Bloomington. That Mr. Neff possesses the abilities of a successful politician is strongly assured by his achievements already made. Born Oct. 26, 1846, he was less than 29 years old when elected

to his present important office. Two years earlier he was
a candidate for Congress in the then Ninth District in com-
petion with the Hon. J. P. C. Shanks, and received, beyond
doubt, a majority of the votes. But the contest was so
close that Mr. Shanks, a Republican, had the advantage in
Congress, to which the decision was referred by Gov. Baker,
and held his seat. In the last campaign upon the stump,
Mr Neff was a full match for Mr. Curry, his antagonist,
who was the champion debater of his party. They met
before the same assemblies, and the popular judgment sustained this view. Mr. Neff possesses the elements of popularity in a high degree in personal intercourse, is shrewd
and discreet in all his movements and very effective as a
political orator. Perhaps the only objection that can be
laid at his door is the circumstance that he is still unmar-
ried, thus setting before the young men of the State, a bad
example in high places. But as it is not yet too late, it is
to be hoped that this mistake will be speedily remedied.

WILLIAM W. CURRY,

SECRETARY OF STATE—OUTGOING,

Was born in Louisville, Kentucky, February 15th, 1824.
His genealogy is American on both sides so far back as he
can trace his ancestry. All the education he was able to
acquire was through the medium of the common schools.
At an early age he was apprenticed to a cabinet maker
and served five years. When twenty-one he entered the
ministry of the Universalist Church, since which time he
has had charge of congregations in Columbus, Danville, New Albany, Logansport and Terre Haute. For

several years past, however, he has divided his time between the pulpit and the stump. In 1864 he made a spirited canvass for Congress in the New Albany district, but in as much as he had a most popular opponent, (Mr. Kerr), both politically and personally, and an overwhelming majority to overcome, it is hardly necessary to add that he did not go to Congress on that occasion. There is no doubt that he came nearer going than any one else of his political principles could have gone. In 1868 he was made a member of the Boad of Directors of the State Prison South and served four years. He was elected Secretary of State in 1872, from which position he recently retired with the well earned plaudits of all parties. Governor Hendricks complimented him highly in his message. He was ably assisted in his official duties by his daughter, Miss Cory Curry. Mr. Curry is universally recognized as one of the most ready debaters and able stump orators in Indiana. Very few have the hardihood to meet him in joint canvass. He has a way of arranging statistics and raining them down upon an opponent like shots from a Gatling gun. His sallies and repartees usually arouse an opponent to manifest displeasure, in which respect Mr. Curry is not wholly unlike the gods who first make mad whom they would destroy. He is a stauch Republican and an ardent advocate of temperance and morality. Though he is now out of office he is still a citizen of Indianapolis.

EBENEZER HENDERSON,

AUDITOR OF STATE—INCOMING.

Mr. Henderson is not the traditional self-made man. He had a good start, and it is as much to his credit, and possibly more so, that a good fortune inherited from his parents, did not make a fool of him as it would have been to have climbed out of poverty by hard work. Both results prove that a man is made of good material. He was born in Morgan county, where his elegant home, property and business interests still remain. The date was June 2, 1833, and he is consequently 42 years old, in the flower and vigor of manhood. He is the only child of parents who came from Kentucky to this State in 1831. He is also a son, but not the only son, by some hundreds, of the State University at Bloomington. There is a fitness in this circumstance, that the State fitted him for her own service. Being possessed of a handsome estate from his father, it was both natural and wise that Mr. Henderson should give that his attention instead of running off to a profession because he was fitted for it by native talent and education. Happy will it be for Indiana when more of her well educated sons shall devote their energies to industry, and crown labor with intelligence and mental culture. Besides farming on a large scale, Mr. Henderson has given a great deal of attention to dealing in stock, and is one of the leading pork packers of the State. His own county honored him in 1860 with the custody of her funds as Treasurer, which duty he discharged faithfully one term. In 1868 he was a member of the State Senate, and one of its active workers. He is a shrewd and effective manipulator of the political tides and currents and makes a sure thing of what he undertakes. In his late campaign he was the nominee of both the Independents and the Democrats, and was strongly supported by both parties. He possesses in a large degree, the elements of personal popularity, especially among the body of the working people. He brings to the duties of his important office as Auditor of State, a wide and extended business experience, a clear record of integrity and great energy ; in short all the elements which guarantee success and honorable service for the State.

JAMES A. WILDMAN,

AUDITOR OF STATE—OUTGOING,

Every inch of Mr. Wildman, and there are about seventy-five of them in the clear, is Hoosier. He was born in the State, grew up on the Indiana plan, not of finance, but of hard, honest labor, and he represents in his character and style the true Western man. A gentleman in every sense, he acts on the rule, without any exception, to treat every other man as a gentleman. This habit, united with a genial and cordial temper, has made him as popular with the people as a man can well become. The people like Mr. Wildman, for he is one of them. No elevation of official position can make him forget the days of manual labor, or divorce his sympathies from that class among whom his career began. He is a native of Jefferson county, born May 22, 1834, of American parentage, and received his education in his own county, beginning on the puncheon-floor of the common school house, and finishing off at Hanover College. He spent a couple of years in Iowa, 1855–6, and then came back and set his stake in Howard county. when Kokomo was a crude and muddy town. He has seen a wagon with one milk can mire down in front of his own door; helped to lay the first flat stone sidewalk, put some money in every one of her churches, built or helped build her fine school, and in short been a part and parcel of that now thrifty and bright city.

Twice elected County Auditor, he developed in that office the qualities which the event has proved fitted him so well to oversee the financial economy of the State. In 1868 he represented his county in the Legislature, and in 1869 was made Grand Master of the Independent Order of Odd Fellows, in which fraternity he stands among the first. He leaves the office of State Auditor with the unqualified approbation of all, irrespective of party. Mr. Wildman is a staunch Republican, always working squarely in the traces, but committed to a fair fight, and in public service treating all alike impartially as citizens of equal rights. In a campaign he is not by any means negligent of political tactics, and as a hand-shaker he has few equals and no superior. It is not time yet to sum up his public service for he is always conspicuous in a crowd, and may get hit again. Indeed, it will be strange if he does not. But whether in public service or in private life, he will honor the State which claims him, and never lack a host of friends.

BENJAMIN C. SHAW,

TREASURER OF STATE—INCOMING.

Was born at Oxford, Ohio, February 3d, 1831. His parents were natives of North Carolina and Ohio respectively. His educational opportunities were confined to an old log school-house, and the first twelve years of his existence in his native State, where in his thirteenth year, he was apprenticed to a carriage maker, and in due time learned that trade and has followed it closely and successfully ever since, except during a part of the period of the war, when he was in the army. From April 1861 until July, 1863, between which dates he served his country as 2d and 1st Lieutenant, Captain and Major of the 7th Indiana, camp commander of the 4th Congressional District, and Lieut. Colonel of the 68th Indiana regiment. He came to the State in 1848, since which time he has resided at Rushville, Laurel, Wabash, Greensburg and Indianapolis respectively. He has been a Democrat all his life, except the eleven years intervening between 1854 and 1865, and he was elected by Democrats and Liberals to the office he now holds, at the last election.

JOHN B. GLOVER,

TREASURER OF STATE—OUTGOING,

Was born in Orange county, Indiana, March 4th, 1833. His parents were both natives of this country; his father removing to Orange county from Kentucky, in October 1814. He was reared on his father's farm in his native county, goinng to school when the weather forbid working in the field. When approaching maturity he attended school at New Albany and elsewhere. After completing his course, he secured the situation of teacher in New Albany, and afterwards taught in the Salem High School. At the beginning of the war he organized a company and was assigned to duty in the 38th infantry. He was elected Captain of the company, and was promoted to Major of the regiment, and he served in that capacity until the war was over. Upon his return from the army his services received recognition by his being elected to the office of County Treasurer. At the close of his term he was re-elected. In 1872 he was elected Treasurer of State by the Republicans, of which party he has been a life long member. He was defeated as a candidate for re-election, and but recently retired from that office to the regret of all his personal friends in Indianapolis and in Indiana, regardless of party.

CLARENCE A. BUSKIRK,

ATTORNEY GENERAL OF STATE—INCOMING,

Is a native of New York. He was born in the beautiful little village of Friendship, Allegheny county, Nov. 8th, 1842. His father's family were descended from Holland, and his mother was of Scotch and Irish ancestry. The son received the rudiments of his education at Friendship academy in his native village. Then he came West and completed his course of studies in the University of Michigan. Having read law with Messrs. Balch & Smiley at Kalamazoo, and attended law lectures at Ann Arbor, he was admitted to the bar in 1865. The year ensuing, he removed to this State and located at Princeton. His legal ability and admirable social qualities soon gave him a first place in the hearts of the people of that section of the State. In 1872 he was nominated for a seat in the Legislature, and was elected. He served on the Judiciary and other important committees, with credit to all concerned, through the special and regular sessions, as appears by the reports. Suffice it to say that he served the State so satisfactorily in that capacity that he was nominated in 1874 for the more responsible office of Attorney-General. Again he was elected and by a large majority. In politics he has always been a Democrat, and an able and ardent champion of the principles of that party. Personally he is a man of imposing appearance and engaging manners.

JAMES C. DENNY,

ATTORNEY GENERAL—OUTGOING.

Was born in Knox county, Indiana, August 8th, 1829. His father was from Kentucky, and his mother from Tennessee, the former removing to this State in 1804, and the latter in 1818. The elder Denny was Clerk of Knox county from 1852 to 1860, and was re-elected in 1860, but under the ruling of the Supreme Court, that such clerks could only hold two terms, he could not serve. He then entered the army as Captain of Company E., 51st Indiana Infantry, but died the same month he was assigned to duty.

General Denny was educated in the common schools of Knox county. in private schools and in the University of Vincennes. He was reared on his father's farm. When about of age, however, he entered a store in Vincennes and remained there as clerk for four years, reading law at night, the last two years, of his service there. Then he secured the situation of deputy county clerk, and read law two years longer. Soon afterwards he was admitted to the bar and began the practice of his profession, having Judge Judah for a partner. The partnership lasted six years, being dissolved by mutual agreement in 1860. Since then he has been judge of the Circuit and Common Pleas Court and Attorney General, from which office he recently retired. During the time since the dissolution above alluded to, when not in official position, General Denny has resided in Vincennes and practised his profession. He makes his home in Indianapolis now ; has an office on Washington street and resides on North Tennessee.

2

JAMES H. SMART,

SUPERINTENDENT OF PUBLIC INSTRUCTION—INCOMING,

Was born in Center Harbor, N. H., in 1841. He received an academic education in the East and came West about twelve or thirteen years since. In 1863 he was engaged in a responsible position in the Toledo public schools, where he taught two or three years Then he removed to Fort Wayne, and was elevated to the superintendency of the schools of that city, and soon became identified with the educational interests of the State at large; so much so indeed, that when the Democratic party had an opportunity to elect a Superintendent of Public Instruction they selected him as the favored one. He had then long been an active member of the State Board of Education, where his rare executive ability was first recognized and appreciated. Those who know him best claim that his strong point is in organization, a quality that eminently fits him for the office of Superintendent of the schools of the State. The ability he displayed in the management of the Fort Wayne schools augurs well for the educational interests of Indiana for the next two years. Added to other good qualities he is an indefatigable worker, never wearying of well doing in his chosen profession. He has labored incessantly to fit himself and others, for the responsible duties devolving upon those who have the responsibility of training the young.

ALEXANDER C. HOPKINS.

SUPERINTENDENT OF PUBLIC INSTRUCTION—OUTGOING.

This gentleman, son of the late Hon. Milton B. Hopkins, was appointed by Governor Hendricks, the successor of his father as Superintendent of Public Instruction in August, 1874. Previously to his father's death he had been engaged in the office, and thereby had become familiar with all its duties and details of business. In the completion of the annual report on the public schools of the State, he has given to the public one of the most valuable documents ever issued on the subject in Indiana. In all the duties of the office, he has been faithful and untiring in the service to which he was called, under circumstances peculiarly sad. Mr. Hopkins is professionally an educator, having been identified with the Howard College at Kokomo and before that had charge of the Ladoga Academy. He was born in Rush county, Nov. 11, 1843, but educated in the University at Lexington, Ky. He returned to Indiana in 1870, since which time he has been an assiduous worker in the cause of education, achieving therein an honorable distinction. Mr Hopkins is a scholar, excelling in mathematical studies, and is also a good singer and musician. In his personal relations, he is genial and courteous to all, and will leave the position to which he was so unexpectedly summoned in the possession of universal respect.

SAMUEL H. BUSKIRK,

CHIEF JUSTICE OF THE SUPREME COURT,

Is an Indianian of noble birth, his family one of the oldest and best in the State. His father was an associate Judge of the Court, and Postmaster of Bloomington under the administration of President Van Buren. The Judge was born at New Albany, January 18, 1820. The first twelve years of his life were whiled away on a farm. There he laid the foundation for the fine physical health he has since enjoyed, and served as a superstructure for his superior mental attainments. His education was acquired in the State University. When he had completed the classical course, he read law and graduated from that department of the same institution of learning. His career in the literary and law departments was an honor to himself and a credit to the college. His public services have been many and valuable to the people of the State. He has been instrumental in making and interpreting the laws under which the people of the State have been so prosperous for more than a quarter of a century. The Judge was a member of the Legislature during the sessions of 1848, 1851, 1855, 1863 and 1865. He served as Speaker in 1863. The reports of proceedings during these various terms are replete with with his words of wisdom. When not engaged in the discharge of the duties of office, he has been practicing his profession in the courts of this and other States; for his reputation as a lawyer was not bounded by State lines. In 1872 he was nominated for Supreme Court Judge by the Democracy, of which party he has been a life long member, and was elected by a majority that was flattering, the closeness of the contest considered. For two years he has been upon the Bench. In that time he has rendered some of the most important decisions ever delivered in the State, notably that concerning mixed schools. His decisions are based upon firm conviction, supported by most exhaustive research into the authorities bearing upon each case that comes before him. Popular clamor nor any other outside influence can swerve him from his high resolve to be right though the heavens fall.

HORACE P. BIDDLE,

SUPREME COURT JUDGE—INCOMING,

Is a native of Ohio, and is about sixty-two years of age. Since 1836 he has been a citizen of Cass county. He lives on an island in the city of Logansport. To reach his residence one must cross, not one, but two Wabash rivers, for here this frisky old stream, as if enamored of the valley, opens its arms and embraces a portion and holds the emerald gem upon its bosom. The place is known to cultivated people as the island home of Judge Biddle. That gentleman is, in many respects, a most remarkable man. For thirty-five years he was prominently before the public. and as popular as prominent. From 1846 to 1852. and again, after an interval of eight years, from 1860 to 1872. he served the Eighth Judicial District as Judge of the Circuit Court. On the occasion of his last election. he received every vote cast for the office, having no opposition, for there was not even a politician who was so wholly devoid of discretion as to appear before the people to contest the honor with him. He was a member of the Constitutional Convention of Indiana in 1850, and participated prominently in the proceedings of that able body. In 1857 he was elected to the Supreme bench, though, through a misconstruction of the law by the executive, he never received his commission.

When not engaged in the discharge of the duties of office Judge Biddle has been busy in the practice of his profession, with marked ability and marvelous success. Three years ago he abandoned active professional life, resolute in his determination to enjoy the comforts of his sunny home, free from the cares and perplexities that attach to business· This resolution was only shaken by the nomination of two State Conventions (Democratic and Independent) for the Supreme Bench, to which he was elected last October, by a majority unprecedented in the annals of Indiana politics.

Then, Judge Biddle is known to fame as an author. Besides being an extensive contributor to leading newspapers and magazines, he published in 1858, a volume of poems; in 1860 a treaties on the Musical Scale, with a revised edition; in 1867 a scientific work, purchased in copyright by Oliver Ditson of Boston, and held as a standard work; in 1868 another volume of poems, with a second edition of the same in 1872, in 1871 "A Review of Professor Tyndal's work on Sound," and in 1873 a large volume of poetry entitled "Glances at the World," besides many other poems and prose productions that take high rank in literature.

ALEXANDER CUMMINS DOWNEY,

SUPREME COURT JUDGE,

Was born of English and Irish parentage, near Cincinnati, Ohio, September 10, 1817. With his parents he removed to this State when quite young. Indiana was then in her infancy, and of Judge Downey, it can truly be said, he grew up with the western country; and he and the country are alike creditable to each other. He worked on his father's farm in summer, until eighteen years of age, attending the district school in winter. About the age of eighteen he enjoyed the rather exceptional advantage of attending the County Seminary. Then he learned a trade which he followed for a time. Possessing an active mind he drifted into journalism and ascended to the editorial chair of a newspaper. Afterwards he read law. In 1844 he settled at Rising Sun, and his star ·of destiny began to a ascend the horizon of his ambition. In 1850 he was elected Judge of the Circuit Court, and served with distinction, until 1858. Meanwhile he was Professor of Law at Asbury four years. He was elected· State Senator in 1862 and served the succeeding four years, and was one of the first Commissioners of the House of Refuge. In 1870 he was elected to the Supreme Bench, and entered upon the discharge of the duties of that position the ensuing year, and he is yet an honored as he is a honorable member of that distinguished body of jurists. Judge Downey is what he has been all his life, a conscientious and a consistent Democrat, from principal and not from policy.

JOHN PETTIT,

SUPREME COURT JUDGE,

Was born at historical Sacketts Harbor, in the State of New York, July 24, 1807. He traces his genealogy to the Scotch and those antagonistic antecedents, English and French. He was educated in the Academy of New York, and through studies prosecuted by himself. The Judge removed to this State in 1831 and he has been part and parcel of its government, legislative and judicial, pretty much all the time. His has unquestionably been the busiest life ever led by an Indianian, at home or abroad. From 1835 to 1839 he was a member of the Legislature of this State; for three years he was United States District Attorney; then he spent six years in Congress as a member of that body from Indiana; was then a member ot the Constitutional Convention; elector at large for President of the United States; three years United States Senator, and Circuit Judge several years; Judge of Supreme Court of Kansas two years. and mayor of the city of Lafayette. In 1870 he was elected to the Supreme bench of this State for six years and is now serving in that capacity, with credit to himself and honor to all concerned. Probably no man in the country is clearer headed on the law bearing upon any case that comes before him than Judge Pettit. His decisions are based upon the law and the evidence weighed in the balance of Justice, and are seldom reversed by the Court above. He has been a Democrat all his his life and has held all the positions of prominence enumerated, through the power of that party, elective or appointive. But his decisions have never indicated party bias.

JAMES L. WORDEN,

SUPREME COURT JUDGE,

Was born in Berkshire, Massachusetts, May 10, 1819. His parents were of English extraction, but of American birth. When the Judge was a mere child, his parents removed to Portage county, Ohio, and he received the rudiments of his education in the common schools of that State. He had a strong, clear, logical mind, and steady, studious habits, upon which to base an education, and an ambitious and impulsive spirit to impel him to excellence in whatever profession he should settle upon for a life's practice. The profession of law, if successfully prosecuted, required those qualities in the eminent degree possessed by him, and he happily hit upon that profession.

His taste as well as talent, led him into law. Having qualified himself for practice, in two years' reading, in Cincinnati, he opened an office at the early age of twenty-two years. After a year and a half spent in that city, however, he resolved to remove to Indiana for the practice of his profession. So 1844 found him established in Whitley county, this State. He had not been there long until his talent was observed and appreciated. He was elected Prosecuting Attorney several terms in succession. In 1853 he was appointed, by Governor, Wright Judge of the Tenth Judicial Circuit, and at the ensuing election he was elected to that bench. Subsequently he was appointed Judge of the Supreme Court by, Governor Willard. The ensuing election he was elected to that position by the people for the term of six years. When that term of service had expired he resumed the practice of his profession, entering into a copartnership with Judge Morris, of Fort Wayne. In 1870, after having enjoyed six or seven years of successful practice, he was nominated for the position of Supreme Judge by the Democratic State Convention, and was elected by a large majority, and he took his seat for six years in October, 1871, and by virtue of that call of his constituency, he is still on the bench in the full and deserved enjoyment of the confidence of the bar and people of Indiana.

ANDREW L. OSBORNE,
EX-SUPREME COURT JUDGE—OUTGOING,

Was born in New Haven county, Connecticut, May 27, 1815. He was educated in his native State, and removed to Indiana in 1836. Having learned the law, he located at Laporte, for the practice of his profession, which he pursued with ability and success until 1844, when, having turned his attention to politics, he was elected to the Legislature. After having served the term through he was re-elected. When that term of service had expired in the Lower House, he was elevated to the Senate. In 1857 he was elected Judge of the Laporte Circuit (the 9th Judicial District). He served until 1863, when he was re-elected. His term of service expired in 1869. In 1872 he was appointed Judge of the Supreme Court, which term of service expired on the 16th of January, 1875. Last fall he was a candidate before the people on the Republican ticket and for the same position. He was defeated by Judge Horace P. Biddle. Politically Judge Osborn was an old line Whig, until the disintegration of the party—then and since a conservative Republican. However, he was never influenced an iota in his opinions, when on the bench, by party considerations.

JAMES BUCKLEY BLACK,

SUPREME COURT REPORTER,

Is a New Jersian by birth. He was born at Morristown, July 21, 1838. His parents were natives of Ireland. He came to Indiana in 1846. Since then he has resided in Wabash, Hartford City, Winchester, Camden, Bluffton, Muncie, Greencastle and Bloomington. He was educated at Asbury University and Indiana State University, at Bloomington. He commenced teaching school when sixteen years of age, and thus acquired the necessary means to defray his expenses at college. During the last term of his junior year the flag was fired upon at Fort Sumpter. His spirit of patriotism asserted itself over his ambition then, and he enlisted as a private in the Union army, in response to the first call of President Lincoln for volunteers. He did not long remain in the ranks however, for he was promoted from time to time until he held the commission of Lieutenant Colonel before he had served the three years and eight months that he was in the army. In 1868 he was elected Supreme Court Reporter, and he is holding that office now. He published the Indiana reports from volume 30 to 45 inclusive. In politics, he has always been Republican, and by profession, a lawyer.

CHARLES SCHOLL,

CLERK OF THE SUPREME COURT,

Was born in Cologne, Prussia, December 27th, 1832. He was educated at the Royal Institute at Munich. At the age of nineteen, liberal political views entertained and expressed by Mr. Scholl forced him into exile. He determined to come to this country, where every man has a right to think and express his thoughts, and at the same time receive the respectful attention of his fellow men, instead of official ostracism. So Mr. Scholl sailed for America, and landed in New York, Nov. 21st, 1851. His landing there marked a new epoch in his life. He was then on free soil, and in a land where a man could carve out his own fortune, untrameled by custom and undisturbed by the minions of royalty. He remained in New York and Newark, N. J., but two years, then removed to Indiana. Settling in Washington county, he taught school for a season. Then, in 1860, he engaged in business at Henryville. Subsequently he was elected trustee of Monroe township, Clarke county, for four successive terms, and Clerk of the Supreme Court in 1872, and is still in office, giving general satisfaction.

WILLIAM BAXTER.

THE SENATOR FROM WAYNE,

(Subject to the contest case with Jeffers) was born in York-shire, England, February 11th, 1824, the same county in which were born John Wickliff, "the morning star of the Reformation," Captain Cook, the daring navigator, William Wilberforce, the brilliant advocate of the abolition of slavery, and also the birthplace of the ancestors of George Washington, and of Constantine, the great Roman Emperor. Mr. Baxter was born of English parentage, and is of the same lineage as the eminent non-conformist divine, Richard Baxter, who was imprisoned in the reign of Charles the First, because he would not conform to the established Church, not even when they offered him Bishopric; the same Richard Baxter who, while he was in prison, wrote the "Saints' Everlasting Rest," and "The Call to the Unconverted." William Baxter, the subject of this sketch, was educated at the grammar school of Burnsall, in the division of Evanen, in the West Riding of Yorkshire. While yet a young man, not liking the monarchical form of government prevalent in England, Mr. Baxter left his native land for the United States, being enamored of free institutions, and ours especially. Before leaving, however, he took an active part, with Richard

Cobden. John Bright, George Thompson, Henry Vincent, and many other reformers, in battling against the iniquitous corn laws, in favor of the repeal of the oppressive game laws, and for the disestablishment of the Established Church of England. It was in February, 1848, that Mr. Baxter left the land of his nativity for the land of his adoption, arriving in America after an uneventful voyage.

Upon his arrival in America, Mr. Baxter traveled through the country on a tour of observation for nine months, and then he embarked in business as a wool merchant on Market street in the city of Philadelphia, which business enterprise he prosecuted successfully for fifteen years, amassing quite a competency. In 1856, he married Miss Mary Baker of Wayne county this State and in 1864, retired from business in Philadelphia and moved to Wayne county, and purchasing a farm near Richmond, engaged in rural pursuits. To use his own language: "Seeing the blighting influences of intoxicating liquors upon men, society and the nation, threatening the disruption of civilized society and the ultimate destruction of my adopted country, I have for the past ten years been devoting my energies to the removal of that accursed traffic from our midst; and believing that we never can put down intemperance by moral suasion alone—any more than we can put down any other great public evil, simply by moral suasion—I have been earnestly advocating the paramount necessity of Legislative restriction on the traffic in alcohol. It was in order to accomplish this that in 1872, I consented to become a candidate for the General Assembly of our State and it was while a member of that General Assembly that I introduced the bill which is now better known as the Baxter Law. This is the only public position I ever held and that single term satisfied my political aspirations. I would prefer never to hold another public office. I was elected to the State Senate at the last election but it was thrust upon me. I would much prefer the privacy of my farm to the Halls of Legislation."

Mr. Baxter is a Republican in politics. His father was a minister of the Wesleyan Methodist Society for nearly forty years in England, and died there.

JAMES RUFUS BEARDSLEY,

SENATOR FROM ELKHART,

Was born in Ohio, of American parentage, in 1829. With his parents he removed to Indiana in 1830, he being but one year old at that time. His father was the founder of the town of Elkhart. The son was educated in the common schools of the county. When he had arrived at the age of maturity, he engaged in the manufacture of flour and paper, and he is now the principal proprietor of the well known Elkhart paper manufactory. He knows how to apply the business principles that achieve success in individual transactions to the treatment of public affairs. This is the second term that he is serving as Senator, which would indicate that his constituents have confidence well founded in him. When he shall have served the ter through, they will no doubt honor him further, unless the people hold him responsible for the many misdeeds of the Republican party, of which he has been a prominent member since its organization.

DANIEL ROBERTS BEARSS,

SENATOR FROM MIAMI AND HOWARD.

Was born in Geneseo, Livingston county, New York, August 25, 1809. His parents were English. Mr. Bearss was educated in the common schools of Western New York, and Detroit, Michigan, and has since been engaged in farming. He came to this State in 1828. Since then he has lived at Fort Wayne, Logansport, Goshen. and resides at present, as for a long time past, near Peru. He has been honored by, and has honored, the people of that section of the State many times. He has held the office of School and County Commissioner two or three terms each. Twice has he been elected to the lower branch of the Legislature, and thrice to the Senate. Originally he was a Whig in politics, then a Republican. and lately a Granger. His son is now a member of the House of Representatives for Kosciusko and Fulton. So it would seem that the genius of office-holding has been handed down from father to son.

ROBERT C. BELL,

SENATOR FROM ALLEN,

Was born in Clarksburg, Decatur county, this State, July 13, 1843. of American parentage, both parents having been born in Kentucky. and having removed to this State in early life. Senator Bell was educated in the common schools, at the Academy at Muncie, and in the law department of the University of Michigan. He served his country as a soldier in the 134th Regiment Indiana Volunteers during the latter part of the late war, and subsequently in the civil service at Nashville, Tennessee, in 1867 and 1868, as Assistant United States Attorney for Indiana, then United States Commissioner for the District of Indiana. For the last two years he has been Attorney for the county of Allen, and a member of the firm of Coombs, Morris & Bell, Fort Wayne. In political principles Senator Bell claims to have been born and bred a dyed in the wool Democrat, and for the last fifteen years has fought the power of darkness in the shape of Radicalism without fear, favor, affection, reward, or the promise or hope thereof. Now he proposes to fight it out on this line if it takes him a life time.

ANDREW J. BOONE,

SENATOR FROM BOONE AND CLINTON,

Was born in Preble county, Ohio, July 17, 1820. His parents were of German and Welch extraction, but both were born in Ohio, and removed to this State in 1827, first locating at Union, and living there until 1833, when they moved to Rush county. Residing there until 1838, they took up their abode at Lebanon, Boone county, where the Senator has since resided. Mr. Boone is a direct descendant of Daniel Boone, the pioneer of Kentucky, he of historical renown. During the earlier days of his life, Mr. Boone was a farmer and a miller, subsequently studying law, first having acquired an admirable education through the common schools, and a two year's course in Indiana University. In that Institution, he was a schoolmate of the late and lamented Prof. M. B. Hopkins, and many others, of Indiana's elder and noblest sons. Like Mr.

Hopkins, Mr. Boone devoted much of his life to the training of the "hope of the State," teaching in several seminaries, notably, Lebanon and Leavenworth. Having learned the law at an earlier date, Mr. Boone did not proceed to practice his profession until 1851, the same year that he married Miss McLaughlin, making it a very eventful epoch in his history. Securing a large practice, he devoted himself too assiduously to the discharge of his duties, and in less than a decade he had so materially impaired his health that he had to abandon his profession and return to his first love—farming.

Not content with the quiet of rural life, he resumed the practice of law in partnership with Hon. R. W. Hanna four or five years afterwards, taking a six or seven mile walk, for exercise, each day. By proper precaution he recovered his health, and is now a hale and hearty man. In politics he has always been a Democrat, and has held many positions of trust and profit through the popular partiality for him. In 1841, he was elected Auditor of the county, and held the office for a term of two years. Being elected Assistant Clerk of the House of Representatives Indiana Legislature in 1849, he was retained in that official capacity until 1852, thoroughly familiarizing himself with the routine of Legislative labor. Elected to the Senate in 1872, he is still the incumbent of that office, and serves both parties to their satisfaction.

Senator Boone is emphatically one of the self-made men of the State, a genuine Western production, and one whom we should all be proud to honor. His father before him, was a prominent personage, having served in the Legislature. The Senator lives at Lebanon, where he is

3

known of all men and universally esteemed for his many good qualities. When the history of Indiana has been written it will not be complete unless one chapter at least, is devoted to the Senator from Boone and Clinton.

JOHN A. BOWMAN,

SENATOR FROM WASHINGTON AND JACKSON,

Was born in Blount county, East Tennessee, April 7, 1818. His father was a native of Virginia, his mother of Pennsylvania. Both the grandfathers of the subject of this sketch served as soldiers in the revolutionary war. As early as 1824, Mr. Bowman came to this State with his parents, having spent two years in New Orleans and one in Pennsylvania previously. What education he was able to acquire was in the common schools of his adopted State. He began business for himself as a farmer and a horse and mule trader, when he was but eighteen years of age. For years, he was in the habit of taking two or three droves south every season, and selling them in the States of Alabama, Mississippi and Louisiana. Indeed, he continued in this branch of business until the breaking out of the civil war and the unhealthful heat of the climate that resulted therefrom. He took but little part in the war until the Morgan raid, when he came to regard it as a part of his funeral as it were, then he raised a company and assisted in securing that daring depredator. In politics he has ever been a Democrat of the unswerving kind, and still adheres to the old Jeffersonian principles. He was elected to the House of Representatives in 1857, without opposition, and in 1859 he was re-elected. So well did he serve

as Representative, his constituents elevated him to the
Senate in 1864, where he represented Washington and
Harrison counties; and in 1872 he was re-elected, and
again without opposition. For fifteen years he has held
office almost constantly, and was never defeated when a
candidate. Under the new apportionment he serves the
counties of Washington and Jackson.

Senator Bowman is a bachelor, and his address is Salem,
Washington county.

WILLIAM BUNYAN,

SENATOR FROM NOBLE AND LAGRANGE,

Was born in Saratoga county, in the State of New York,
October 20th, 1833. His parents were of American birth
and Scotch descent. Mr. Bunyan was reared on a farm,
and continued to work upon it until he was twenty-
four years of age; then he engaged in trade, thus
amassing a competency. The only educational advantages
he ever enjoyed were the district schools in the vicinity
where he resided during boyhood. In 1854 he came West
and grew up with the country in and around about Lima,
for four or five years; then he removed to Kendallville,
where he has resided for the last sixteen years. During
the short and stormy period of his more mature manhood,
he amassed quite a competency in a worldly way, and
can well afford to devote a part of his time and talent in the
illy-paid service of the State. Before he was elected Senator, in 1872, Mr. Bunyan had never held any position of
trust or profit through political preferment. He is now,
and has been since the organization of the party, an ardent

Republican. When he shall have served through the session, Senator Bunyan will retire to private life, conscious of having, to the best of his ability. discharged the duties of his position with a view of doing the greatest good to the greatest number.

PETER CARDWELL,

SENATOR FROM HAMILTON AND TIPTON,

Was born in Rockingham county. North Carolina, December 20, 1825. His parents were of English descent, and they removed to Hamilton county, this State, in 1829. Senator Cardwell is a self-educated man, and follows the occupation of a farmer and stock-raiser. In early life he was thrown on his own resources and though almost penniless, educated himself to the extent of being qualified to teach school for several years. He served as a School Trustee in 1864, and was an appraiser of real estate in Hamilton county in 1869. During the war he became Captain of a home company, and thus served until the close of the war. Formerly a Republican, he now glories in the political freedom of an Independent. He may be heard from by addressing him at Noblesville.

CHARLES W. CHAPMAN,

SENATOR FROM KOSCIUSKO AND WHITLEY.

Was born at Richmond, Indiana, September 19, 1828. His father was American born, but of German extraction; his mother was born and reared in Ireland. Mr. Chapman

has always resided in Indiana; at present at Warsaw.
The foundation of his education was laid in the common
schools of his native county, and completed, so far as a collegiate course could accomplish it, in Asbury University.
By profession he is a lawyer, and has been more or less
prominent in the politics of the State. Early in the war
he entered the army, and ascended to the colonelcy of the
Fourth Indiana volunteers. In 1861 he was elected Representative, and Senator in 1864. He was then appointed
Register in Bankruptcy. He is now a Senator, having
been elected to that position in 1872. A Whig until the
disruption of that organization, he has been a Rupublican
since.

R. H. CREE,

SENATOR FROM MADISON AND DELAWARE,

Was born in Warren county, Ohio, December 24, 1820.
He traces his lineage back to Ireland, though his parents
were of American birth. In 1841 he came to this State,
settled down in Madison county and began business as a
farmer and dealer in live stock, having only enjoyed the
advantages of the common school system of Ohio and
Indiana. Politically he was a Republican until the rank
corruptions of that party drove him from it, and then he
became independent in politics. In the last campaign the
Independents nominated him for the Senate and the
Democracy indorsed the nomination, Williams, their candidate, withdrawing, that the two parties might unite on
and thus insure the defeat of the Republicans and the
election of "an anti-Administration, anti-Morton, and an

anti-Pratt Senator," as a local paper put it. For a time a contest case was canvassed, Mr. Cree's opponents claiming the seat for Orr, who had been chosen to fill out the unexpired term of a deceased member. After a careful reading of the Constitution and mature reflection, they concluded it would end in smoke if attempted, and they therefore abandoned the project, only having hope in the first place of being able to take advantage of a technicality to defeat the will of the people and the ends of justice. Senator Cree's postoffice address is Alexandria, Madison county.

WILLIAM CULBERTSON,

SENATOR FROM RIPLEY, OHIO AND SWITZERLAND,

Was born in Switzerland county, December 16, 1827. His parents were from Scotland, but America was the land of their adoption. Mr. Culbertson was educated at home. After he had completed his education he served an apprenticeship at blacksmithing, and followed that business until 1870, when he engaged in the art agricultural. He has been a resident of Switzerland county all his life, except during two or three years, some twenty years ago. In 1860 he was elected Justice of the Peace, and held the office one year, resigning to enlist in the army. On the organization of the 140th regiment, he was commissioned captain of Company B, and so served until mustered out in 1865. Politically Mr. Culbertson was a Whig until 1861, since when he has been a Democrat. He was elected to the Senate in 1872, and is yet a member of that body, by virtue of his election. Near Moorefield is where he resides.

ADDISON DAGGY,

SENATOR FROM PUTNAM AND HENDRICKS,

Was born in Augusta county, Virginia, February 26th, 1824. His parents were Gorman-Americans. The Daggys settled in Putnam county, when he was but twelve years of age. After attending the schools at Greencastle for a season, the son entered Wabash College, at Crawfordsville, where he subsequently graduated with honor to himself and credit to his class. Then he read law, and for the last twenty-four years, has practised that profession, sixteen years of that time as the junior member of the firm of Williamson & Daggy, Greencastle, one of the best known and most successful law firms in Western Indiana, Mr. Williams, the senior partner, having once served the State as Attorney-General. In 1832 Mr. Daggy was elected Prosecuting Attorney for the Common Pleas Court of Putnam and Hendricks and acted in that capacity for two years. He represented Putnam in the lower house of the Indiana Legislature, session of 1867–8. In 1872 he was elected to the position he now holds, as Senator from Putnam and Hendricks.

In politics Senator Daggy was a Whig while that party was in existence ; a Republican now and ever since the abandonment of that old organization.

JASPER DAVIDSON,

SENATOR FROM POSEY AND GIBSON,

Was born in Pike county, Indiana, October 13, 1838. His parents were natives of Virginia, and removed to Indiana in 1861, and settled in Gibson county. Mr. Davidson received none but a common school education. Having acquired that, he taught the young idea how to shoot in winter, and in the summer trained the aboriginal cereal to tassel, and performed other rural duties. He has been a Democrat all his life, and a member of the Methodist church, and yet he has never darkened the door of a saloon or indulged in the noxious weed. He also has the honor of raising the best wheat in Gibson county—43 bushels to the acre—last season.

DAVID DARWIN DYKEMAN,

SENATOR FROM CASS AND CARROLL,

Was born in Wayne county, New York, January 16, 1833, of English and German parentage, and has lived in Indiana over twenty years past, having resided for a short time in Kentucky and Iowa. He received his preparatory education at that staunch old Methodist seminary in Cazenovia, New York, which has sent out armies of brilliant students. His finishing course was had at Falley University. His residence is in Logansport, where he stands among the foremost lawyers of the place. For five years he held a seat in the common council of the city, and was on the bench of the Common Pleas Court three years. Politically he is a life member of the Democratic party, and an active worker in public affairs. Judge Dykeman is a man who relies wholly on his own resources, is nervous, fiery, plucky, and never holds still for his enemy to pound him. In personal appearance he is one of the finest looking men in the Senate, with a clean, smooth face, fair complexion, and firm lip. He speaks readily, distinctly and agreeably. He is among the leading spirits of the Senate, disposed to be fair, positive and earnest. It takes but little to wake him up, for he is not apt to be caught very sound asleep, and it is not advisable to tread too carelessly or heavily on his corns. Being only forty-two years old, and a diplomatist in politics. it is not to be presumed that either his ambition or career will end in the State Senate. It is plain enough to be seen that his political history is mainly yet to be both made and written.

GEORGE W. FRIEDLEY.

SENATOR FROM LAWRENCE AND MONROE.

Was born in Harrison county. Indiana, June 1, 1839, of German and Scotch parentage. He resided with his parents on the farm until he was sixteen years of age, and then in Bartholomew until the war, when he enlisted in the 69th regiment, Indiana volunteers, and served therein until its consolidation with the 24th regiment. He served in the latter regiment until the close of the war, with the exception of a period during the siege of Vicksburg, when he was engaged on the staff of General Burbridge. He also served on that of General Richard Owen, a part of the time. After the Vicksburg campaign, he was elected Colonel of the consolidated regiment, there being but two dissenting voices. It was decided that there was no vacancy, however, and Colonel Friedley never received his commission. He participated in the capture of Fort Gaines and the storming of Fort Blakely, Mobile Bay, in 1865.

Mr. Friedley was educated at Hartsville University, and

read law, and is by profession and practice, a lawyer. In 1870, he was elected to the lower House, from Lawrence county, and in 1872, to the Senate, and he is now holding over, by virtue of that election. He has always been a radical Republican and does not now give up the ship. As a candidate he has heretofore been successful in every instance. His address is Bedford, Lawrence county.

JONATHAN HENRY FRIEDLEY,

SENATOR FROM SCOTT, JENNINGS, AND DECATUR,

Was born in Harrison county, Indiana, April 25th, 1827. His father was of German and his mother of English and Irish descent. The elder Friedley was once Postmaster at Comargo, Jefferson county, and is now Postmaster at Woostertown, Scott county, where the son receives his mail. Senator Friedley, was educated in the district schools of Harrison and Jefferson counties. Though the facilities were not first-rate he secured an average education. He began business as a farmer and a miller, but of late years has been at the head of the leading store of his adopted village. He is always head-centre in Church and Sunday school movements in the M. E. denomination, of the same place. He has been a member of the Methodist Church ever since he was fifteen years of age, and for more than a quarter of a century has sustained the relation of a Steward. In the meantime he has been Class Leader, Sunday School Superintendent, Trustee and Delegate to National, State and County Conventions of Church and Sunday School. He has also always been a teetotaller and an advocate of the temperance reform. He has ever taken a deep interest in his country's welfare, and has never been ashamed to work openly and above-board for his political principles, holding his country in his affection next to his God, standing up for that which he believed to be right, against all that seemed to him wrong, whether in politics or religion. He is also an avowed champion of reform and retrenchment. He served in the Senate in 1872 in the interest of Scott and Jennings He claims to be one of the people, and, while not seeking office, he seeks to serve the people and let the office seek him.

H. C. GOODING,

SENATOR FROM VANDERBURGH.

Was born at Greenfield, Indiana, June 14, 1836. His parents were American-born. His grandfather on his father's side, Colonel David Gooding, of Kentucky, commanded a regiment from that State in the famous fight known as the Battle of the Thames, and the men under his command claimed for him the distinction of having taken Tecumseh's scalp, about which there have been so many accounts, each at variance with all the others. The Colonel died in Madison county, this State, several years since. Senator Gooding's father, Asa Gooding, was a hotel keeper and merchant in Greenfield up to the time of his death, in 1842. The Senator, himself attended school there for a while and then entered upon a classical course at Asbury University which he completed in 1859. Upon graduating, he read law and settled down to the practice of his profession in Illinois. When the war broke out he enlisted as a private but before he had been long in the service he was promoted to Adjutant and acted as Judge Advocate. At the close of the war he practiced law in Washington for a season. Then he moved to Evansville, where he has lived and practiced his profession ever since. In 1870, he was nominated by the Republicans of that district to run against the Honorable W. E. Niblack for Congress, his opponents before the convention being Colonel C. M. Allen, General Laz. Noble of Vincennes, Judge Asa Iglehart of Evansville and other prominent politicians of the "Pocket" and "Old Post." He was defeated by Mr. Niblack, as any one would have been. In 1872, he was elected Senator and served through both regular and special sessions. He is a brother of the Hon. Dave S. Gooding and General O. B. Gooding and a nephew of the late M. B. Hopkins, our lamented Superintendent of Public Instruction. His political principles are Republican.

JOHN BRIGHT GROVE,

SENATOR FROM BROWN AND BARTHOLOMEW,

Was born in Augusta county, Virginia, August 22d, 1829, and was cradled in the lap of luxury of the F. F. V.s so to speak His ancestors were Irish and German. He was educated at Shemariah Academy. University of Pennsylvania, and read medicine until he had perfected himself for the practice of that profession. In his time he has held many positions of prominence under the government, State and national, besides many others of trust and profit. In 1849 he was surgeon of the good ship Ralph Cross, from Philadelphia to San Francisco, and upon his arrival at the

Golden Gate City he was appointed Inspector of Customs for the said city. Then for sixteen months he was resident physician to the Yuba County Hospital, situate on the Slope. This was in 1856 and 1858, including a part of each of these years. In 1862 he was post surgeon to the Union army at Marshall, Mo. After the war he settled at Columbus, and in 1871 and 1872 he was a member of the Common Council of that city from the Third Ward. It would seem that Senator Grove enjoys the confidence of the powers that be—both elective and appointive—in a large degree. In politics he has been a Democrat since the old line Whig organization disorganized. He was elected to the Senate by the Democracy, but represents all the people, the just and the unjust alike. His home is in Columbus.

ELIJAH HACKLEMAN,

SENATOR FROM HUNTINGTON AND WABASH,

Was born at Cedar Grove, near Brookville, Indiana, October 18, 1817. His parents and grandparents were of American birth. but his great grandparents were natives of Germany. Abraham. father of Elijah Hackleman, was a native of North Carolina. He removed to Scott county, Kentucky, in 1802, and in 1807, came to what was then known as a part of the Territory of Indiana, now Franklin county. During the war of 1812. he served as a Federal officer. In 1821. he moved to Rushville, though the town was not then laid off. At that time, this was the extreme settlement and the West was an unbroken wilderness. With his trusty ax he here began at an early age to carve out his own fortune. The narrow limits of educational facilities peculiar to pioneer time did not prevent his acquiring an education. He mentally devoured all the books accessible and it was often said of him that he was never known to be without a book in his pocket even when at work, availing himself of every opportunity to stock his mind with its contents. When nearing the age of maturity the sire saw that the son was not cut out for a hewer of wood, etc, and sent him to school at the Connersville Seminary where he soon became quite proficient in mathematics and astronomy. He was for sometime a student of the Honorable Benjamin F. Reaves and read law with General P. A. Hackleman, his cousin, now deceased. In the earlier days of his manhood Senator Hackleman taught school and acted as Justice of the Peace. In May 1849, he moved to Wabash county and improved a farm through habits of industry acquired in earlier life. He has been in his time elected County Surveyor, twice receiving every vote cast, in the county for that office. Twice elected Clerk of the Circuit Court, he served to the satisfaction of all. At the last election he was elected to the Senate from Wabash and Huntington by the Republican party. a member of which he has been since the disruption of the Whig party.

JAMES F. HARNEY.

SENATOR FROM MONTGOMERY.

Is a native of Shelby county, Kentucky. He was born March 1. 1824. His father was of Scotch and his mother of German descent. They came to Indiana and located at Ladoga in 1825. The father was a minister of the gospel, of the Christian or Campbellite denomination, and a well educated and cultured gentleman. He was a brother of T. H. Harney, of the old Louisville *Democrat*. Senator Harney, the son, was educated at Wabash College, taking a thorough classical course, something very rare in those days. At the incipiency of the Mexican war, he volunteered in the service, and was assigned to duty in the First Indiana. Upon reaching Matamoras, on his way to the front, he was stricken down by disease, and was forced to return on account of continued ill health. "Misfortunes never come singly," as he realized through an awful affliction, which he sustained in the meantime, losing his father and only brother by well damp. This calamity left his widowed mother and four children solely to his support. This impelled him to engage in something for the speedy support of the surviving members of his father's family, and he became a manufacturer of woolen goods at Ladoga, where he still lives. But being a man of magnificent mind and personally very popular, he was elected to the Legislature in 1849, also in 1858, and again in 1862. During these various terms he served with such distinction that he was elected to the Senate in 1872, and by virtue of that election is now here serving in the Senate during the pending session. He is known as an able speaker, fluent and logical. From the first, he has voted uniformly with the Democratic party.

RICHARD M. HAWORTH,

SENATOR FROM FAYETTE, UNION AND RUSH,

Was born in Union county, Indiana, October 14, 1821, His father was of English, and his mother of Irish descent, the former having been born in Tennessee and the latter in North Carolina. They removed to this State about the year 1814. Senator Haworth did not enjoy the advantages accruing from a collegiate course, but made the most of his opportunities, and managed to receive a good English education in the common schools of his native county. By occupation he is a farmer. In 1860 he was elected to the Lower House of the Indiana Legislature, and State Senator on the Republican ticket in 1872, and is now holding over; when his time shall have expired he will have served the State six years. In politics he was a Democrat in early life, but principle led him to espouse the cause of the Liberty party, and he became a Free Soiler, and subsequently a Republican. Throughout all his public and private life Mr. Haworth has been found in advance of the age in movements for the improvement of the minds and the morals of man. The spirit of independence and justice which impelled him to desert Democracy in the interest of the enslaved, also led him to champion the temperance cause, and to take advanced grounds in educational matters. He lives at Liberty, Union county.

JOSEPH HENDERSON,

SENATOR FROM ST. JOSEPH AND STARKE,

Is a native Indianian. He was born in Wayne county, near the town of New Port, July 6, 1829. His father and mother were from North Carolina; emigrated to Indiana at an early day. His father died while he was about ten years old. His mother lived until about ten years ago. He was a student for a while under Barnabas C. Hobbs, at Richmond, in said county. Shortly after leaving said school he entered Wittenberg College at Springfield, Clark county, Ohio, and remained in said college for several sessions. He taught school some after leaving college. While teaching school at Marion, Grant county, he commenced the study of the law under the Hon. Isaac Vandervanter, a prominent young lawyer of that town. After spending a summer in Marian he emigrated to South Bend, St. Joseph county, where he now resides. He continued the study of law at his adopted home in the office of Judge Elisha Eebert, now deceased, who was one of the *purest* and *best* men that ever lived. He also attended a law class taught by the Hon. Thomas S. Stanfield, several winters in succession. Judge Stanfield is known to the people of Indiana as one of her ablest Judges. He was a partner for several years of the late lamented Norman Eddy. He was elected to the House of Representatives in 1870; re-elected in 1872; elected to the Senate in 1874. He was born in the Democratic church, but he was never radical on any subject. His address is South Bend, St. Joseph county, Indiana.

JAMES B. HENDRICKS,

SENATOR FROM WARRICK AND PIKE,

Is a native Indianian and not ashamed of his nativity. He was born in Hanover, Jefferson county, May 25, 1840. His father was a prominent Presbyterian preacher of the

4

old school, and the son received a careful training. He was
educated in the common schools and engaged in the drug
business, in which he has been eminently successful.
Though he never aspired to political position, he was nominated by the Democracy of Warrick and Pike last fall and
elected by the vote of men of all parties, being a man of
personal popularity. However, he has always been a Democrat of liberal tendencies. Personally the Senator is
affable and agreeable. Petersburg is his post office address.

WILLIAM RUFUS HOUGH,

SENATOR FROM HANCOCK AND HENRY,

Was born on the 9th day of October, A. D. 1833, in the
village of Williamsburg, Wayne county, Indiana. He is
the eldest son of Alfred and Anna Hough. His father is a
native of Surrey county, North Carolina, whence in
the year 1813, at the age of three he emigrated with
his father, Ira Hough, who was a prominent member of
the Society of Friends, to the territory of Indiana, and
settled at New Garden, in Wayne county. The mother,
whose maiden name was Anna Marine, is a native of
Marlboro District, South Carolina, and is the daughter of
the late Rev. John Marine, who, together with his family,
emigrated to the State of Indiana, and settled in Wayne
county about the year 1823. Senator Hough resided in
his native village until he was eight years of age, when
with his parents he removed to Hagerstown, in the same
county, where they remained about one year. In the fall
of 1842, they emigrated to what was then known as the

"St. Joe Country," arriving on the first day of November at the village of Middlebury, in Elkhart county, where they still reside. His opportunities for obtaining an education were such as were afforded by the common schools of the villages in which his parents resided. the "Middlebury Seminary," and a few months' study in the "La Grange Collegiate Institute," which was originally chartered as a manual labor school, located at Ontario, La Grange county, Indiana. The leisure hours of his school days he occupied principally in assisting his father in the prosecution of his business, cabinet making, finishing furniture, painting, etc.; but having determined, when but a boy, to adopt a different avocation, he didn't take enough interest in it to "learn the trade." He taught school two terms in La Grange county, the last of which was during the winter of 1855–6, and left the home of his parents during the following summer to "try his fortune in the world." In the latter part of the same year he began the study of law in the office of Captain R. A. Riley. in the town of Greenfield, the county seat of Hancock county. While prosecuting his legal studies, he was, without solicitation on his part, appointed to the office of School Examiner of Hancock county, and having performed the duties of that office to the satisfaction of the Board of Commissioners for one term, at the expiration thereof he received the appointment for a second term, which he accepted, and again satisfactorily discharged the duties of the trust. Then he began the practice of his profession.

In the fall of 1860 he was elected District Attorney for the judicial district comprising the counties of Hancock, Madison, Henry, Rush and Decatur, almost without opposition, and faithfully discharged the duties of said office

for one term, at the end of which he resumed and applied
himself zealously to his professional business, with a view
to building up his home practice, confining his labors to
his own county principally. Yet he has made a reputation
as a lawyer that is known and envied throughout his section of the State, combining the qualifications of counsel
and advocate. He is possessed of a good share of financial ability, which has enabled him to so husband the proceeds of his practice that, although he is yet comparatively
a young man, he has accumulated an amount of property
that would by most people be regarded as a competency,
and he is at this time one of the largest tax-payers
in Hancock county. He has never been an office-seeker,
but has since attaining his majority been an active
member of the Republican party. As a citizen and a legislator he has been an ardent supporter of our free school
system, and in favor of the adoption of such measures as
will the most rapidly develop and perfect the same, believing the individualizing effect of education upon the
citizens of a free government essential to its perpetuity.
He served industriously during the special session of 1872,
and the regular session of 1873 of the General Assembly,
and during the latter session was a member of the following Standing Committees: On Education, Benevolent
Institutions, State Library, Claims, Organization of Courts,
Rights and Privileges of the Inhabitants of the State, and
on the Joint Committee on State Library and Claims, on
all of which he was characterized by ability and faith-
fulness to the trusts of his position. He is serving on
several important committees this session.

WASHINGTON IRVING HOWARD,

SENATOR FROM STEUBEN AND DE KALB,

Was born in Jamaica, Windham county, Vermont, May 7, 1837. His remote ancestors were English, but his parents were both of American birth. The foundation of Senator Howard's education was laid at Leland Seminary, in the State of Vermont; then he graduated from Darmouth College, and read law. In 1854 he removed to Iudiana, and located at Angolia, where he practiced the profession of law until a short time preceding his election to the Senate, when he engaged in the sale of hardware. From 1863 to 1867, however, he was treasurer of Steuben county. His father was for several terms a member of the Vermont Legislature, and for forty years a Justice of the Peace in that State. Office holding, therefore, is not wholly unknown to the family circle of the Howards. Senator Howard was a Democrat until the organization of the Republican party, when his political faith underwent a marked change, and he has been a member in good standing of the Republican party since. His home is in Angolia, Steuben county.

ANDREW HUMPHREYS,

SENATOR FROM DAVIESS AND GREENE,

Was born in Anderson county, Tennessee, March 30, 1821. His father was a native of Tennessee, and his mother of Virginia. He moved to Indiana in 1827. Senator Humphreys resided for a season in Putnam county, and then removed to Linton, Greene county, where he now lives.

He received a good common school education, the best that could then be had without the expenditure of a great deal of money, for that article was not so plentiful then as now. As early as 1849 Mr. Humphreys was elected to the Legislature, and was kept there by his constituents in some capacity until 1857. Two years afterwards, in 1859, President Buchanan appointed him Indian Agent for the Territory of Utah, and he so served until 1861, at which date he resigned, and returned to his home in Indiana. Senator Humphreys has always been an ardent Democrat, and in times of great political excitement, violently so. He is a man of strong convictions, and resolute to assert the principles he conceives to be right. He regarded the rebellion as a revolution ; and, conceding the South's right of secession, he desired that those sister States should pass out of the Union at pleasure and in peace. When not in office the Senator from Greene and Daviess, tills the soil of the latter county.

FRANKLIN CONSTANTINE JOHNSON,

SENATOR FROM FLOYD,

Was born at Constableville, Lewis county, New York, June 23, 1836. He is the second son of Judge Horace Johnson, a well known lawyer and jurist, and also a prominent Democratic politician of Central New York, now and for many years a resident of Syracuse. Mr. Johnson was educated at the academies of Lowville and Rome, in his native State. Leaving New York in 1852 he came direct to Indiana and attended the first State Fair, at

Indianapolis. There he got a glimpse of the varied and vast resources of our State, and he resolved to add one to its population by locating in it. So he settled in New Albany and engaged in business as a clerk in the whole-sale hardware establishment of Brooks & Brown, and was thus employed until he had attained the age of twenty-one years, when he became a member of the firm of Brown, Johnson & Crane. He continued a partner in the business of that firm until 1861, when he sold his interest in the concern to purchase the Southwestern Nurseries, of which he is now and has since then been the proprietor. He at once became identified with the horticultural and agricul-tural interests of Indiana, and has been active in their advancement ever since. He has been for many years Vice-President of the State Horticultural Society. In 1871 he was commissioned by Governor Baker to represent Indiana at the organization of the National Agricultural Congress at Nashville, and in the ensuing year was chosen a member of the State Board of Agriculture. Last year he was re-elected. In January, 1873, he was nominated by Governor Hendricks as one of the Indiana members of the Centennial Commission, and in February he was commissioned by President Grant. In May Mr. Johnson attended the first annual meeting of the American Cheap Transportation Association in New York, as the represen-tative of the National Agricultural Congress, and assisted in its organization, besides otherwise prominently partici-pating in its organization. This, coupled with the addi-tional circumstance of his having organized more Granges in Indiana than any one else, must in a measure account for the fact that in June ensuing he was ousted from the Centennial Commission to give place to General Passenger

Agent Boyd, of the Pennsylvania Railroad Company, who had not been a citizen of the State since early boyhood. And, added to the above enumerated incentives for casting Mr. Johnson off the Centennial Commission, is the fact that a year ago last summer, in answer to a letter from Senator Wyndom, inquiring into the grievances of the farmers of this State, he (Mr. Johnson) in behalf of the agricultural classes of Indiana, stated such grievances succinctly and strongly, and he then avowed himself in favor of the establishment of a Bureau of Commerce and Transportation, providing for a Commissioner from each State, selected by the State Legislature in joint session, thus vesting the power of control within easy access of the people.

In politics Senator Johnson is a Democrat, and has been such all his life. In 1870 he was elected to the City Council of New Albany, and served two years in that official capacity. At the Cincinnati Convention in 1872 he represented the New Albany district and supported the lamented Greeley, first, last, and all the time, and upon returning home he urged the claims of that gentleman on all who loved honor in high places, most warmly and ably, until the close of the canvass.

JAMES T. JOHNSTON,

SENATOR FROM PARKE,

Is a native of Putnam county, this State. He was born January 19, 1839. His parents were natives of North Carolina, and removed to Indiana in 1820. They settled in Washington county, but did not remain there more than two or three years. They then located in Putnam county. The date of their settlement there was anterior to the laying off of the town of Greencastle. In 1861 the senior was Sheriff of the county. Senator Johnston was educated in the common schools of the county, and read law in the office and under the careful instruction of Williamson & Daggy. This was in 1860–'61. Hardly had he completed his course of reading when he felt called upon by the most vital interests of his country to bear arms in her behalf, and he responded by enlisting in Company " C," 71st Indiana. He served in that regiment until 1863, when he was transferred to the 8th Tennessee cavalry, where he was commissioned Lieutenant. Subsequently he was Quartermaster Sergeant of the 133d Indiana, a one hundred day regiment. When his term of service therein has expired he became Quartermaster of the 149th Indiana. In September, 1865, he was mustered out of the service and returned home. The year following, he removed to Parke county and located at Rockville and engaged in the practice of the law. He is now a resident of Rockville and a member of the legal firm of Rice & Johnston, and in the enjoyment of a remunerative practice. For two years Senator Johnston was Prosecuting Attorney for the Parke, Vigo and Sullivan Circuit. In politics he is a Republican, living in the very Gibralter of the party in Indiana.

JOHN M. LA RUE,

SENATOR FROM TIPPECANOE,

Was born near Harrison, Hamilton county, Ohio November 24, 1826, of French and German descent, his father, however, having been born in New Jersey, and his mother in Pennsylvania. Mr. La Rue resided in Hamilton county, Ohio, until September 30th, 1830, when he removed to Tippecanoe county, this State, where he has since resided. Taking a course in Asbury University, he graduated in 1849. Subsequently he studied law, and, having acquired that profession, has been practicing for many years. In 1856 he was elected to the Lower House, from Tippecanoe county, and served satisfactorily through the term. He was chosen Common Pleas Judge in 1868 and served satisfactorily until the abolition of that office, in March, 1873. Mr. La Rue is Republican in politics and has been since the disorganization of the Whig party, to which organization he had before belonged, only deviating from it to support Van Buren, the Free Soil candidate, yet not voting, knowing it would do no good, inasmuch as he (Van Buren) could not be elected. Senator La Rue lives in Lafayette, and is regarded as one of the leading citizens of the Star City.

GEORGE MAJOR.

SENATOR FROM BENTON. NEWTON, JASPER AND WHITE,

Was born in Hamilton county, Ohio, September 18, 1819. His parents immigrated to Pennsylvania from Ireland before the Revolution, and removed to Hamilton county, Ohio, in 1816. The father of the subject of this sketch never held office, but his brother, Andrew, has represented Carroll and Clinton in the Senate, and Clinton in the Lower House, of the Indiana Legislature. The son was educated at private school, and removed to this State in 1831 and settled in Clinton county, where he continued to reside until 1864, when he removed to Jasper county, where he has since lived on his farm. Politically, he was educated a Jackson Democrat; voted for Van Buren, Polk, Cass and Pierce; opposed the repeal of the Missouri compromise; took part in the anti-Nebraska movement in 1854; voted for Fremont and Lincoln, and supported the administration of the latter during the war of the rebellion; he was dissatisfied with the McCulloch financial policy and favored the nomination of Pendleton in 1868, but eventually voted for Seymour: in 1872 he was a delegate to the Cincinnati Convention, and supported Trumbull, but voted for Greeley and the Democratic State ticket at the polls; at the inauguration of the independent movement he took a prominent part, and was elevated to his present position by the Independents. In a district that had before given a Republican majority of eight hundred, Mr. Major was elected by six hundred and sixty-two votes. He resides at Remington, in Jasper county.

JAMES JAY MAXWELL,

SENATOR FROM MARION AND MORGAN,

Was born in Morgan county, Ind., February 27, 1839. His parents were Irish and Scotch, respectively. His father was born in Ireland, and came to this country when he was but six weeks old. His mother was reared in the Highlands. Mr. Maxwell has lived all his life between the two Indian creeks, and all he knows he learned at home, never having enjoyed to any considerable degree the advantages

of the school system of the State. The first vote he ever
cast was for Douglass and the Democratic ticket in 1860,
but during the war he acted and voted with the Republicans,
regarding that organization as the party of patriotism. In
1872, after having seen the Republican party outlive its
mission and its usefulness, he became a Liberal and supported the noblest Republican of them all for the Presidency,
though the ticket on which he run was a mixed one. He is
now opposed to the administration of public affairs by the
Grant dynasty. During his whole life Mr. Maxwell has
been a farmer, and can conscientiously claim to have acted
honorably in his dealings with his fellow men. In fact his
relations with those who have had business to trans-
act with him have been so amicable and agreeable
that he has never had a suit at law. If the world were all
like Mr. Maxwell the law would be the poorest profession
in all the land, whereas it is the most remunerative. Winchester is Mr. Maxwell's address.

ANDREW J. NEFF,

SENATOR FROM WAYNE,

Was born in Preble county, Ohio, November 30, 1825;
parents of German descent; the father from Pennsylvania,
the mother from Maryland. In 1839 Mr. Neff came to
this State and settled in Wabash county, then moved
to New Castle, thence to Hartford, and subsequently
to Winchester, where he now resides. He was educated at
the academies in New Castle, Muncie and Winchester, and
read law with Judge Bundy ; was appointed Circuit Pros-

ecutor by Governer Wright, in 1855, and in 1856 was elected Representative from Blackford county. Early in the late war, he enlisted in the service in the capacity of Major of the 84th Indiana volunteers; was promoted to Lieut. Colonel, and subsequently Colonel, and finally Brevet Brigadier General by Andrew Johnson, then President. In 1864, his term of service in the army having expired, Mr. Neff began to publish and edit the Journal, at Winchester, and continued so to act until 1869. In 1872 he was elected to the Senate from Randolph county, by the Republicans, with whom he had been acting since he left the Democratic party in 1858; and he is now holding over. For his services to the State during his legislative career, the reports of the various sessions through which he has served, speak in terms of glowing praise. His war record is a part of the history of the country. Winchester is Mr. Neff's address.

DANDRIDGE HALLADAY OLIVER,

SENATOR FROM MARION,

Is a Kentuckian by nativity, but an Indianian by adoption. He was born in Henry county, Kentucky, November 11, 1822, and came here in October, 1836. He is a worthy son of a noble sire, and bears as a given name the maiden name of the worthy wife of the father of his country. His grandfathers fought for the liberties we enjoy through the well won victories of the Revolutionary war, participating with particular prominence in the decisive battle of Yorktown. His father, John H. Oliver, wore the eagles in the militia service for many years, besides serving his country as a postmaster. Upon the occasion of the lamented Statesman, Henry Clay, visiting Indianapolis, when his (Clay's) star of destiny was a blaze of glory, the elder Oliver was a most prominent member of the committee of reception. The son studied medicine, and after having acquired as good an English education as could be had in the schools of this section of the State at that time, having read the books prescribed by his professional adviser, he attended and graduated from the medical department of the University of Louisville, winning honors for himself and credit for his class. Then he commenced to practice, and at once began to reap a rich harvest of business in reward for the care he had taken to first thorougly qualify himself.

During the war, while he did not go to the front and fight, as his brothers did with great credit to the family fame in military matters, he performed professional service in the families of soldiers gratuitously. In that way he served his country to a greater advantage than had he drawn the sword in her defence. Politically, Dr. Oliver was formerly a Whig, now a Republican. In 1872, he was elected to the State Senate, and is serving as such still.

HENRY A. PEED,

SENATOR FROM MARTIN, DUBOIS AND ORANGE COUNTIES,

Was elected by a majority of two thousand two hundred and twenty-five on the Democratic ticket, the principles of which party he always professed and practiced. He had served the State as Representative for the counties of Martin and Dubois, having been elected to that position in 1872, serving in special and regular session on the Committee of Ways and Means. Mr. Peed is of English and Scotch extraction; having been born in Johnson county, Indiana, seven miles northeast of Franklin, November 9, 1845. Educational facilities in that neighborhood in those days were limited to an old log school house, and the elder Peed's means being limited, the subject of this sketch could only receive a common school education, which, however, he made the most of. Mr. Peed worked on his father's farm until the breaking out of the war of the rebellion, and then he shouldered arms and served his country in the army of the northwest, as long as his services were required. Then he returned to this State and repaired to Columbus, where he located, and there he learned the art preservative, in the office of the Union, meantime reading law with G. W. Richardson, of Hill & Richardson. Having acquired both professions, his fortune was made. Leaving Columbus he went to Martin county and established the Herald, in 1868, since which date he has devoted his time and talent to the practice of the profession of law, and editing the Herald, making a large, general and local reputation, especially as an editor.

In politics Mr. Peed is now and always has been a Democrat. He never held office but once until elected to the Legislature, and then was School Examiner of Martin county, for one year. The postoffice address of the Senator from Dubois, Orange and Martin, is Shoals, Martin county.

WILLIAM P. RHODES,

SENATOR FROM FOUNTAIN AND WARREN,

Was born in Tippecanoe county, July 17, 1833. His father was of German and his mother of English and French descent. He was educated at Fort Wayne College, and read law. He made his home in Tippecanoe county until 1859, and then removed to Williamsport, Warren county, and entered upon the practice of his profession. In the winter of 1860, he removed to Kankakee, Illinois, but returned again in the ensuing spring and resumed his practice. During the war he served in the 135th Indiana Volunteer Infantry, as Captain of Company K. At the close of the war he returned to Williamsport and resumed the practice of his profession there. In 1870 he was elected to the Lower House of the Legislature, and discharging the duties of the trust to the satisfaction of his constituency, he was elected to the Senate in 1870, and is now holding over. He is Republican in politics.

MORGAN BRYAN RINGO,

SENATOR FROM OWEN AND CLAY,

Was born in Henry county, Kentucky, March 23, 1818. With his parents, who were also native Kentuckians, Mr. Ringo removed to Indiana in the spring of 1833. In early manhood he identified himself with the agricultural interests of Clay county, where he has lived so long. He has farmed his landed estate with more than ordinary care and intelligence, devoting much of his time to the improvement of his stock, as well as to the improvement of his farm, setting a good example to that large class of farmers who allow their land and stock to become alike impoverished. By industry and intelligent labor and rigid economy Mr. Ringo has accumulated quite a competency. The only educational facilities he enjoyed were in the common schools of Kentucky and Indiana, but he acquired an education of which he should not be ashamed. In 1872 he was elected to the Senate on the Democratic ticket, of which party he has been a member since 1860, having been a Whig the twenty years preceding. However, he is very liberal in his views, differing with the majority of Democrats on the temperance question. Poland is his P. O. address.

J. D. SARNIGHAUSEN.

SENATOR FROM ALLEN, ADAMS AND WELLS,

Was born in Hanover, Germany, October 31, 1818. He came to this State and settled at Fort Wayne, in 1862, and has resided there ever since. Before coming to this country he received a college and university education. Mr. Sarnighausen is and has long been a newspaper editor by profession, and as editor of the Staats Zeitung at Fort Wayne, has wielded great influence among his German-American fellow citizens in the community where he lives. In 1870 Mr. Sarnighausen's claims to the Senatorship, for the county of Allen, were urged by the German and American friends he had made by the manly manner in which he conducted his paper. The election was so close that a contest resulted and Mr. Sarnighausen lost his seat, though on the first count he was ahead one hundred and

5

seventy-one votes. Not discouraged, however, his friends prevailed upon him to become a candidate for the counties of Allen and Adams, and he consented. This time he was elected by six thousand one hundred and eighty-four majority, indicating great political and personal popularity. He is a Democrat.

The county of Wells was admitted to the Fort Wayne district under the last apportionment law.

Senator Sarnighausen's father held a high civil office under the former kingdom of Hanover, but notwithstanding the favors royalty heaped upon the sire, the son recognizes the republican as the best form of government the world has ever witnessed.

HARVEY D. SCOTT,

SENATOR FROM VIGO,

Was born in Milford Union county, Ohio, December 18, 1819. His parents were natives of the United States. His infancy was spent in Union, but his childhood days were whiled away in Ashtabula county, a part of the beautiful Buckeye State known as the Western Reserve. In 1838, however, he moved to Indiana, and, as fortunate fate would have it. located in the fruitful valley of the Wabash, at Terre Haute. He was educated at Asbury University, Greencastle, and subsequently became learned in the law. Then he became skilled in politics. He has held, in his time, the office of Prosecuting Attorney one term, County Treasurer of Vigo county two terms, Representative in the Lower House of the Indiana Legislature one term, member of the National Congress one term, and one term State Senator, and he is serving in the latter capacity still. His record of public service is a long one, and one of which neither he nor his constituents are ashamed. During the last session of the Legislature he was generally regarded as one of the ablest members of the higher branch of that honorable body. Politically, he was first an Anti-Slavery Whig, then American, and now a Republican. In private, as well as public life, he has ever been found in the very van of all movements that could tend to the advancement of the moral and mental condition of the community and country. When not engaged in official or professional life, his time, for years, has been occupied in horticulture, at his country residence, in the suburbs of the city of Terre Haute. He is an ardent friend of the agricultural class of the country, and aids in all ways he can to advance their interests. He is more or less identified with the Grange movement through this sympathy. The purity of his private life is one of his many virtues.

DE FORREST L. SKINNER.

SENATOR FROM LAKE AND PORTER,

Is a native of Vermont. He was born in Hardwick, Caledonia county, in 1853. His father was one of the leading lawyers in that State. The son was educated at a private acadamy, and acquired an extraordinarily good English education, his opportunies cons.dered. When but eleven years of age, he came to Indiana with his parents, and had been here but a year when he was bereft of his father by death, and was, at that early age, thrown upon his own resources, and they proved equal to the emergency. His first business venture was in the dry goods line and he at once secured the support and confidence of all with whom he had dealings. His business undertakings have all been crowned with success, and he is now about as well off in a worldly way as any man of his age in Indiana. For many years he has been regarded as a leading spirit in inaugurating movements for public improvement in his section of the State, especially rail road enterprises. He was one of the most extensive contractors for the construction of the Pittsburgh, Fort Wayne and Chicago, Chicago and Lake Huron, and the Cincinnati and Chicago, all of which were successfully built. and are now in active operation. In 1864, his health failing him, he took a trip across the plains, and after having endured many physical privations, and passed through great peril, he returned home in robust health. While absent, he had many adventures with the Indians. He even had the rare satisfaction of reading his own obituary in his home paper; and the joy unspeakable of comforting his estimale wife in her supposed widow- wood. The writer might dwell upon the romance of the Senator's eventful experience, but leaves that to J. Fennimore Cooper's graphic and prolific pen.

Politically and personally, Senator Skinner is very popular in the north western part of the State, as is indicated by his election from such a stronghold of Republicanism as he represent, he being a Democrat. In 1866 he was nominaed by the Democracy of Porter county, for the lower house of the Legislature but was defeated, though he ran far ahead of his ticket. Last fall he received the Democratic nomination for Senator from Lake and Porter, and was elected by a handsome majority, overcoming a

Republican predominence of over eleven hundred votes. The Senator is now in the prime of life, with a flattering future before him. He resides at Valparaiso where he is Vice President and principal stock-holder of the First National Bank, the financial bulwarks of the beautiful and prosperous little city where it is established.

MAJOR ROBERT SLATER,

SENATOR FROM JOHNSON AND MORGAN,

Was born in an old log cabin in Dearborn county, Indiana' January 5, 1833. He is the son of a French Canadian father and a Vermont Yankee mother, and he claims to have been educated in "the wind-shaken garret of dilapidated fortune." By virtue of this education he became a printer by occupation, but he was not destined to stick type all his life. He had a penchant for pushing the pencil ; so in 1859 he began to edit the Franklin Democratic Herald, and has been so engaged, when not in office, since that time. In 1856 he lived in Aurora, and was elected City Clerk. During the administration of Andrew Johnson he was appointed mail agent on the Jeffersonville, Madison and Indianapolis Railroad. Politically he has always been a Democrat of the most ultra type, and was elected to the Senate from Johnson and Morgan by a larger majority than any other Democratic Senator ever received. He served in regular and special session with distinction, holding important positions on committees, and is now a member of the State House Committee from the Senate.

GEORGE B. SLEETH,

SENATOR FROM DECATUR AND RUSH,

Is a native of New York where he was born on the natal day of our Republic, (July 4th,) 1837; His parents were of Irish nativity and had arrived in America but three months before the birth of the son who is made the object of this sketch. When he was nine years of age Senator Sleeth had the melancholy misfortune to suffer the loss of paternal protection, through the death of both his loved and loving parents. For the three succeeding years, he was cared for by friends of the family in Pittsburgh. Then, at the tender age of twelve, he left them to seek his fortunes in the then "far west." It was in 1852, that he first set foot upon Indiana soil, and he stuck to it tenaciously from the start. He first located at Laurel, Franklin county, and followed farming for a livelihood, working for a farmer named Winship. Meantime he neglected no opportunity for the acquirement of an education either in or out of school. Indeed, he never ceased his educational endeavors until he had taken a thorough course in Farmers' College, Ohio. Having thus laid a firm foundation on which to base a profession, in 1862, he entered the law office of the Hon. Leonidas Sexton, (now Lieutenant-Governor of the State and President of the Senate,) at Rushville, where he still resides. There he prosecuted his studies with that intelligence and steadfastness of purpose that has characterized his whole life, and led him from poverty to plenty, and to professional and political prominence. In 1872 he was elected to the State Senate from the counties of Decatur and Rush, and served with marked ability through the succeeding session, and is now a member of that honorable body. He is one of but few men in his profession who would prefer his practice to political preferment, but is willing to respond to the call of his constituents. That the office should seek the man and not the man the office, is one of his firmest convictions. His reputation as a lawyer is the gratification of all the ambition that animates him to strive to obtain and maintain a prominent position in the hearts of the people of his adopted State. As a politician, he is conscientious, and is true to his conscience when an unscrupulous measure of legislation is being urged in the interest of party.

MILO R. SMITH,

SENATOR FROM MARSHALL, FULTON AND PULASKI,

Was born in Logansport, Cass county, July 1, 1820. His father was born near Harper's Ferry, on the old Virginia shore, and his mother in Kentucky. They moved to Indiana in 1810, first locating in Harrison county, and remaining there until 1824, when they removed to Crawford county. Residing there four years, they removed to Cass county, where the father had received the appointment of Government Blacksmith to the Miami and Pottowattamie Indians at a salary of $500 per annum. The elder Smith was a blacksmith during the week, and a Baptist minister on Sunday. He organized the first church of that denomination ever established in Logansport.

Senator Smith's lines of life were not cast in pleasant places, yet he is as " happy as a big sun flower," to use his own happy expression. His father died in 1831. Adopted by his sister, he was taken to Knox county, Illinois, where he was suffered to grow up with the country until 1840, when his sister moved to Galena, taking him along. There and elsewhere, he was knocked about among his relatives until 1846, when he began business for himself as cabin boy on a Mississippi steamer, where his moral education was no longer neglected. Serving two years in that capacity, without being blown up, he returned to Indiana and abided at Rochester for a season; then settled in Logansport and sold goods there for eight years. He returned to Rochester in 1856, where he has since resided. His schooling was of that practical character that makes the man. Senator Smith is a lawyer, and practices that profession when not engaged in the service of the State.

STROTHER M. STOCKSLAGER.

SENATOR FROM CRAWFORD AND HARRISON,

Was born in Mauckport, Harrison county, Indiana, May 7, 1842, of American parentage, both mother and father having been born and reared in Shenandoah county, Virginia. He is now and always has been a resident of Harrison county, his present postoffice address being Corydon. After having taken a course of instruction at the academy near Corydon, Mr. Stockslager entered the Indiana State University at Bloomington, but did not graduate, having to give up his collegiate course. In 1861 he assisted in raising a company for the 13th Indiana Volunteer Cavalry; and in 1864 entered the service himself as 2d Lieutenant of the same company, and he served with such skill as secured for him promotion to the captaincy of the company, in which capacity he served until the conclusion of the war.

He displayed great daring and presence of mind at the battle of Murfreesboro, Tennessee, during Hood's desperate advance in 1864. Mr. Stockslager read law with the Hon. Simeon K. Wolfe, Member of Congress from the Third District; served Harrison county as Deputy Clerk from 1856 to 1860, and as Clerk from 1867 to 1869 He is now, and has always been, a Democrat. His father was the first Democratic Sheriff ever elected in Harrison county, and he served from 1856 to 1860.

WILLIAM CLINTON THOMPSON,

SENATOR FROM MARION,

Is a native of Butler county, Pennsylvania. His parents were born at Philadelphia, of Scotch, Irish and German extraction. His father was a farmer by occupation, and to that avocation he trained the son in early life. But before he had attained his majority, the subject of this sketch suffered the loss of both father and mother, and was thrown upon his own resources; but he was equal to the emergency. He managed to amass means enough to attend school in Cannonsburgh and Pittsburgh, in Pennsylvania .and afterwards to graduate from the Cincinnati Medical College. In 1847 he came to Indiana and located in Indianapolis, and entered upon the practice of his profession, in which he exercised such skill and fidelity as won for him the confidence and support of all with whom he came in contact. Professionally he has been very successful, and the same is true of all his undertakings. This is duly attested by the fine property he has around him, all of which he has earned. In politics the Doctor was a

Democrat until 1850, when he became a Republican, and has remained so since, though he is not the kind of a man to sacrifice principle to party or persons. His record is that of an Independent Republican. For eight years he was a member of the city council, and when he shall have served through this term will have served the State in the Senate six sessions. During the war he was a Brigade Surgeon, and discharged the duties of the trust to the satisfaction of superiors, subalterns and patients. In the beginning he was assigned to duty in the Army of the Potomac, and acted there until after the battle of Antietam, when he resigned on account of failing health. It is not inappropriate to add here that Dr. Thompson has been the family physician of all the Governors of Indiana, from Wright to Baker—quite a distinction, indeed. He has been continuously a citizen of Indianapolis for nearly a quarter of a century, except six years spent in St. Charles, Missouri. The Doctor is a genial gentleman, one whom it is worth a day's journey to meet in social converse.

ROBERT TOBIN,
SENATOR FROM SPENCER AND PERRY.

Was born in Tobin township. Perry county, Indiana, December 17, 1815. His parents were both of American birth, but of foreign extraction. the father of Irish and the mother of German descent The elder Tobin was Judge of the County Court one term, and Justice of the Peace for nearly a quarter of a century. Robert was educated in the common schools of his native county, and after graduating therefrom, he engaged in agricultural pursuits, in which avocation he has spent about all his life to the date of his call to the Legislative halls of the State. However, he had before held several township offices, but they did not interfere with the management of his farm. In politics, he was first a Whig, then a Republican, and is now identified with the Working Men's party, through the influence of which he was elected to the Senate of the State of Indiana. His address is Tobinsport, Perry county.

ISAAC UNDERWOOD,

SENATOR FROM GRANT, BLACKFORD AND JAY,

Was born of Welsh parentage, in Clinton county, Ohio, July 21. 1821. He graduated at the old log school house, and then he turned his back upon his *alma mater*, and engaged in agricultural pursuits—and the pursuit of good bargains in the stock trade. In December, 1856, he came to Indiana, and after sojourning in Randolph county two years and Fort Wayne one year, he settled down to business in Jay county, where he has since lived. In 1861 he represented Jay county in the Lower House of the Legislature. He was once Treasurer of that county. These two positions are the only ones he has hitherto held by political preferment. However, he has held quite a number of responsible positions of a public character. For one year he was Treasurer of the Cincinnati, Richmond and Fort Wayne Railroad, and for a time Vice-President of the Lake Erie and St. Louis Railroad. In politics Senator Underwood was a Whig until the organization of the Republican party, then he joined that party and acts with it still. He is an avowed champion of such legislation as shall result in the greatest good to the greatest number and does not believe that there is any antagonism between capital and labor, and thinks those giant interests would be harmonious were they properly managed.

HENRY M. WILSON,

SENATOR FROM SULLIVAN AND KNOX,

Was born in Greene county, East Tennessee, January 12, 1815, of Scotch parentage; was educated in that State, and removed to Sullivan county in 1831, and has resided there ever since; by occupation is a farmer. Mr. Wilson has held office and played a prominent part in local politics for the last twenty-two years. During that time he served the county of Sullivan as Trustee, Justice of the Peace, School Commissioner, Auditor, Clerk, and Recorder. In 1860 he was elected to the State Senate, and served four years. He was elected by the Democratic party, of course as every official must be who comes from that stronghold of the Democracy. Mr. Wilson has ever been a consistent member of that organization, and was a delegate to the Charleston Convention in 1860. His father was an officer holder before him, having been a Justice of the Peace, Postmaster, etc.

JOHN H. WINTERBOTHAM,

SENATOR FROM LA PORTE,

Was born at Humphreysville, now Seymour, Connecticut, November 13, 1813. His parents were English by birth. but American by adoption. At the time of Senator Winterbotham's birth his father was manager of a woolen manufactory for General Humphreys—Washington's Minister to Portugal, and the first importer of merino sheep. Under the supervision *of the elder Winterbotham, the Humphreys mills turned out blankets and clothing for the army of the United States during the war of 1812. At the close of the war General Humphreys admitted Mr. Winterbotham to the firm as junior partner, which relation was not dissolved until by the death of the General, in 1818. Continuing the business until 1828, Mr. Winterbotham was overwhelmed with business reverses, and became a bankrupt through protective legislation. Then he came West to grow up with the country, locating in the then wild woods of the State of Ohio. It is said that the feeling of all the surviving members of the family is to walk a mile to kick a sheep—or a protective legislator. Owing to these reverses Senator Winterbotham could only graduate from the old log school house in the district where the family settled, near Fredericktown. He spent several years in farming, when he left school, after which he began the sale of agricultural implements through the Western States, for Eastern manufacturers. In 1849 he became the junior member of the firm of Pinney, Lamson & Co., manufacturer of agricultural tools, Columbus Ohio. They contracted largely for convict labor in the Ohio State Penitentiary. In 1853, Mr. Winterbotham sold his interest in, and retired from the firm. Immediately thereafter he formed a copartnership with Gen. G. A. Jones, of Mt. Vernon, Ohio, and with him leased the Iowa Penitentiary for the term of ten years, and engaged in the manufactory of agricultural implements in that institution until the expiration of the lease. Soon afterward, in connection with Gen. C. R. Wever, he established the Fort Madison National Bank, and he was president of this sound financial institution until his removal to Michigan City, where at the earnest solicitation of the Warden and Directors, he contracted for 150 men in the State Prison North, and employed them in the manufacture of cooperage for the Chicago market; also made carriage bodies and gearing, which were sold extensively throughout the United States. In 1871 he made a contract for the service of 200 men in the Illinois State Prison at Joliet, and he is now carrying on an extensive manufactory in the Illinois and Indiana Penitentiaries, under the firm name of J. H. Winterbotham & Sons. He is withal a gentleman of remarkable executive ability, firm, and resolute, and he has been successful in all his undertakings.

He is also a man of marked mental ability, and is descended from an intellectual family. His great uncle, William Winterbotham, will be remembred by literary people, as an author of American history. His works can be found in the older libraries. The Senator's sister, Mrs. Ann S. Stephens, has an enviable reputation as an authorese. During the last session of the Legislature, the Senator served the State with distinction.

DAVID TURPIE,

SPEAKER OF THE HOUSE AND REPRESENATIVE FROM MARION,

Says Lanman's Congressional Dictionary, " was born in Hamilton county, Ohio, July 8, 1829 ; graduated at Kenyon College in 1848; studied law, and was admitted to practice at Logansport, Indiana, in 1849; was appointed by Governor Wright, whom he succeeded in the Senate, Judge of the Court of Common Pleas in 1854, and was Judge of the Circuit Court in 1856, both of which offices he resigned. In 1852 and also in 1858, he was a member of the Legislature of Indiana, and in 1863, he was elected Senator in Congress for the unexpired term of J. D. Bright, and immediately succeeding J. A. Wright, who served by appointment of the Governor."

For years Judge Turpie has been prominently before the public as a politician. At one time he was a candidate for congressional honors, and gave the Hon. Schuyler Colfax an enlivening race, and it was in the palmiest days of that lamented Christian statesman. For sometime he has been a member of the Indianapolis bar. Last fall he was elected to the lower branch of the Legislature. It is an anomoly in American politics that a former United States Senator should consent to the use of his name as a county candidate. Judge Turpie did that because he is a man who holds himself in readiness to go where the people call, without regard to his own personal preferences. Upon the organization of the House, he was elected Speaker, and already he has the members trained to familiarity with parliamentary practice. He is a positive man and one born and bred to command.

SAMUEL AMES,

REPRESENTATIVE FROM LAKE,

Was born in the State of New Hampshire, of English and German parentage, July 14, 1814. He was educated a civil engineer, in New Hampshire, and removed to Pennsylvania in 1838. There he lived until 1856, when he removed to this State. He settled down to farm life in Lake county, near Lowell, and lives there still. Before the present, he has never held any office of prominence in county or State. However, his father was a member of the Legislature of New Hampshire as early as 1824, and served the State with distinction. The gentleman from Lake responds at roll call from the Republican side of the House, but he is not a violent partisan.

JOSEPH HARE ANDERSON,

REPRESENTATIVE FROM TIPPECANOE,

Was born near Fairview, Guernsey county, Ohio, November 15, 1838. His father was a native of Pennsylvania, of English extraction; his mother was a native of Ohio, and of Scotch descent. They removed to this State April 15, 1866. The senior Anderson was for eighteen years a Justice of the Peace, but devoted himself to agricultural pursuits, training his son in that avocation, insisting that it was the surest way of making a living. Representative Anderson, not content with the quiet walks of his father's rural retreat, and inspired by the official career of his paternal progenitor, as Justice of the Peace, worked in the harvest at the age of fifteen years, for means with which to pay his way at school, and pave the way to future greatness. By this means he acquired an average English education, and finally concluded that physicians made it pay, and didn't have hard work to perform, so he studied medicine with Dr. McPherson, of Fairview. Subsequently he took a course in the Cincinnati Medical College, graduating therefrom. In 1862 his country called, and he enlisted in the ranks of the 40th IowaRegiment, but was soon promoted to the medical staff of the 1st Iowa, where he served and dispensed the enlivening pill for eight months, and received another promotion, this time to the General Hospital, where he served until the close of the war. Since then he has been engaged in the practice of his profession at Coburn, Tippecanoe county. He was elected Township Trustee in 1872, and served two years. Dr. Anderson was born and bred a Republican, always lived a Republican, and he expects to fight it out on that line, as he expresses it, in the language of our excellent Executive.

JAMES W. ARNOLD,

REPRESENTATIVE FROM PIKE,

Was born in Warwick, July 4th, 1817. His parents were American and had removed to Warwick county but three years previous to his birth. Schools were scarce when the subject of this sketch was a school boy, yet he managed to secure a very creditable education, the circumstances considered. When with his father on the farm, he worked in the cornfield but at a subsequent period in life. he felt called into the vineyard of the Lord, and for the last few years he has been engaged as a minister of the Gospel. Last October, however, having received a call from the people, he is now serving the State for a season, in the Halls of Legislation. Representative Arnold is a real representative of the true blue Democracy, a credit to the party and the county he is here to serve. Stancel is his post office address.

GEORGE T. BARNEY,

JOINT REPRESENTATIVE FROM NOBLE AND ELKHART,

First optically observed the wonders of this wicked world in New York, April 10, 1822. His parents were also natives of New York. The subject of this sketch came West and located in Ohio in 1837, and there remained until 1844, when he removed to Indiana, and settled at Elkhart. Living there until 1852, he pulled up stakes and pitched his tent in Michigan, and there remained until 1860, when he returned to Elkhart, where he has since continued to reside. In early manhood he graduated from Oberlin College, in Ohio; and, after reading law, he practiced until his health failed him, when he returned to the rural regions and pursued the avocation of a farmer. He has, however, held a number of offices in his time, amongst others that of Constable, Justice of the Peace, Township Assessor, Sheriff, and United States Marshal under President Buchanan. In politics, he is what he always has been—Democratic.

GEORGE RUSSEL BEARSS,

JOINT REPRESENTATIVE FROM KOSCIUSKO AND FULTON,

Was born at Peru, Miami county, November 24, 1834, and of American parentage. He was educated at Kenyon College, but has heretofore followed the avocation of farming, and hitherto has held no official position. His father, however, has been a member of both branches of the Legislature and is now a member of the Senate. In politics Representative Bearss is a Republican. He has resided in Peru and Rochester, but the latter place is now his postoffice address.

T. S. BELLOWS,

REPRESENTATIVE FROM CLARKE,

Was born near Lyme, in the State of Connecticut, November 7, 1816. Mr. Bellows is a direct descendant of one of the oldest families of Yankee land, and can trace his lineage back almost in sight of Plymouth Rock, "on the wild New England shore." Before he can remember, however, he lost his father by death, and when but three years of age he moved to Indiana with his mother. She settled in Clarke county, and there the subject of this sketch has lived since. All the education he ever received was through his own exertions. When he began business for himself, it was as a farmer, and all the money he has or ever had, he earned by the sweat of his own brow. He has held most of the offices within the gift of his neighbors, who know him best. He has served two terms as Sheriff of Clarke county; also, one term as County Commissioner. In politics, he is and ever has been, a sound Democrat. New Providence is his post office address.

GEORGE WORTH BENCE

REPRESENTATIVE FROM CLAY,

Was born in Jefferson county, Kentucky, November 11, 1846, of American parentage. With his parents he removed to Putnam county, this State, November 1, 1853. He worked in the summer on his father's farm, and attended school in the winter, until he had attained the age of 23. Then he read medicine with Dr. Wilcox, at Greencastle. After having read there until he had a fair knowledge of the restorative art, he attended lectures in the medical department of the University of Virginia, until he graduated in 1871. As a Physician, Dr. Bence takes high rank in his section of the State. His course of reading with Dr. Wilcox was a thorough training of itself, to say nothing of his attendance at the University of Virginia, one of the standard medical institutions of the country. Last fall he was urged to accept the nomination of the Democracy of Clay county, for Representative; and at last he accepted, though he was well aware that he had a Republican majority of three hundred to overcome. After making a vigorous canvass, he had the satisfaction of being elected by nearly that majority. As a Legislator, he is making a record that should be satisfactory to his consitutents.

GEORGE H. BROWN,

JOINT REPRESENTATIVE FROM JASPER AND WHITE,

Was born of American parentage, in Jackson county, Ohio, May 11. 1816. When he was but eleven years of age, his parents removed from Ohio to Tippecanoe county,

Indiana. There he was educated in the district school nearest his father's farm, and there he lived until 1840, · when he removed to Jasper county, where he has resided ever since. By occupation he is a farmer and stock dealer. He was born for an office-holder, however, for he had not lived in Jasper county three years before the dear people besieged him with persuasion to serve them as County Commissioner. He consented, and they kept thrusting the honor upon him for a decade. In 1860 he became a Republican in politics, and continued to act with that organization until 1870, since when he has been independent in politics, and was elected to the Legislature on that ticket. Rensselaer is his post office address.

BARKER BROWN,

JOINT REPRESENTATIVE FROM RIPLEY, DECATUR AND RUSH,

Was born in Bourbon county, Kentucky, December 5, 1824. His parents were also native Kentuckians. When the son was but ten months old his parents removed to Indiana. Those were pioneer days, and even log school houses were few and far between. But there was one in the community where the Browns located even then, and to that the subject of this sketch walked in winter, acquiring what was then regarded ·· a right smart education," as that part of the country was a waste a and wilderness. Farming was the fashion in those days as everybody got along in harmony and there was no need of lawyers and newspaper editors and reporters and other disturbers of the public peace. Upon the settlement of the county and the advent of lawyers, Justices of the Peace were a necessity and Mr. Brown was elected. Then as civilization advanced, Legislators were required and now Squire Brown, in response to the call of his constituents in the counties enumerated above, comes to the Capital. The Squire is a Democrat and has been ever since the Whig party "went into Know-Nothingism." His home is at Milroy, Rush county, Indiana. By occupation he is a farmer.

GEORGE BURSON,

JOINT REPRESENTATIVE FROM FULTON, PULASKI AND STARKE,

Was born of American parentage, but Irish descent, in Columbiana county, Ohio, February 24, 1827, and came to this State in 1853. He was educated in the common schools of the State of Ohio, and read law, adopting that as his profession. Since learning the law he has practised his profession, with the exception of two or three years that he spent in the army. In the service he was 1st Lieutenant and then Captain of Co. H. 40th Indiana volunteers, and subsequently was made Major of a regiment of colored troops and assigned to duty in Arkansas, where his health failed him, and in consequence he resigned in the fall of 1863. In 1864 he was elected to the position of Assistant District Attorney of the 25th Judicial Circuit, and served in that capacity, until 1866.

His father was Treasurer of Van Wert county, Ohio, for several years.

In politics Representative Burson has been a Democrat since 1864, but was a Republican before that, after the war began.

FRANK D. CALDWELL,

REPRESENTATIVE FROM CLINTON,

Was born in Butler county, Ohio, of Scotch and Irish parentage, September 13, 1823. He came to this State with his parents in 1830, and first settled in Fayette county, and then in Clinton county, where he has since resided. From youth to manhood he enjoyed one continuous course in "Brush College," and graduated with the first honors of his class. But he bears his honors with becoming meekness. In 1856 he was elected Sheriff of Clinton county, and served to the satisfaction of all concerned, until 1861. When his term of service had expired, he resumed rural pursuits until 1863, when he assumed the editorship of the Frankfort Crescent, and so acted one year. He was engaged in mercantile business at Kilmore, and also in the stock trade for a season. The first office he ever held was that of School Trustee. He was elected Representative in 1870, and again in 1874. Politically, he has been a Democrat ever since the abandonment of the Whig organization, and is now encouraged to always remain such.

JOHN ALEXANDER CANTLEY,

REPRESENTATIVE FROM CASS,

Was born in Monroe county, West Virginia, February 13, 1825. His parents were of German descent. His grandfather, Lincly, was a Captain in the Revolutionary war, and fought with Washington for American independence. Mr. Cantley came to Indiana and stopped in Henry county in 1844. Leaving there five years afterwards, he traveled and taught school seven years in various parts of the State, finally settling down at Logansport, where he served eight years as Justice of the Peace. Originally a farmer, he had but poor opportunities for obtaining an education, but he succeeded admirably under the circumstances. In politics Mr. Cantley is and has ever been a Democrat. He cast his first vote for General Lewis Cass; voted for Douglass in 1856, but wintered his vote in 1872, not having an appetite adequate to the consumption of crow.

DAVID CHARTERS,

REPRESENTATIVE FROM MIAMI,

Was born in Milton county, Pennsylvania, January 25, 1821. His father was of Irish and his mother of German descent. He was educated in the common schools of the old Key Stone State, and adopted the avocation of a farmer for a living. When twenty-three years of age he left the hampering confines of the old homestead and came West in the pursuit of fame and fortune, and he found them both in Indiana. As a farmer he is prosperous, and has the honor of representing the county of his adoption in the Legislature. In politics he was first a Whig, and followed the fortunes of that party to the end, but he is a Republican now. Peru is his postoffice address.

NATHAN HUNT CLARK,

REPRESENTATIVE FROM HAMILTON,

Is a native of North Carolina, as also were his parents. He was born in Randolph county, in that State, September 10, 1825. After attending the common schools of that State and acquiring as much of an education as they could afford him he removed to Indiana and engaged in agricultural pursuits. Mr. Clark is a member and a minister of the religious society of Friends, and a full believer in salvation by and through Jesus Christ, as all his fathers were. Politically he is and all his life has been, a believer in the universal brotherhood of man, and that all men of every nationality, color or clime, ought to have the same right before the law. Therefore he has always adhered to the original Abolition, Free Soil, and Republican parties, and he now avows his belief to be that the salvation of this nation, so far as human agency is concerned in such salvation, depends upon carrying out to its entire legitimate conclusion the great doctrine of the equality of all men before the law. He is therefore still a Republican, and expects to see far more gloomy days than those of 1861 if he lives to see the party that was victorious last fall come into full possession of the the General Government of the United States. He is also an advocate of advanced temperance ideas, and has already offered a bill to further this reform. He lives at Eagletown.

ALFRED B. COLLINS,

REPRESENTATIVE FROM WASHINGTON,

Is a native of Indiana, having been born in New Albany, September 10, 1835. His parents were both natives of Virginia. His father, the Hon. James Collins, represented Floyd county in the Legislature for several sessions, and served as Senator for the same county one term. He also acted as Agent of State for two years, and was well known as an eminent lawyer. Representative Collins was educated at Greencastle, and read law. In March, 1873, Governor Hendricks appointed him Prosecutor for the Third Circuit. In politics Mr. Collins was a Republican until the candidacy of Mr. Greeley on the Democratic ticket, when he observed that about all there was true to Republicanism in the party had left it. Then he experienced a change, and became Liberalised. So when the time came, in 1874, to dispense with the services of the stewards of that party, the Democratic Central Committee of Washington county called upon Mr. Collins and asked him to assist, and tendered him the nomination for Representative. Though he had not sought, and did not desire the distinction, he accepted the nomination, made a most thorough canvass, and carried the county by a handsome majority. He had to contend against a combination of Republicans and Independents, but every effort was made to break the Democratic line without avail. It was the warmest canvass ever made of the county, and as Mr. Collins was the only county candidate experienced in public speaking, the great burden thereof devolved upon him. Mr. Collins resides at Salem, and is a member of the law firm of T. & A. B. Collins.

CHARLES E. CRANE.

REPRESENTATIVE FROM KNOX,

Was born in Wayne county, New York, February 14,
1836. His parents were Americans by nativity. When
the son was but two years of age, the Cranes migrated
to Michigan. When he had attained the age of fourteen he launched his bark upon the waters of life and
began thus early to " paddle his own canoe." Having, by
his own exertions acquired a good general English education,
he taught school in Tennessee, whither he went from Michigan, when he left the paternal roof. By general reading
and persistent application to study he also acquired a fair
knowledge of the classics. In 1861 he felt called upon by
his country to return to Michigan, and attach himself to the
cause of the preservation of the Union. His patriotism
being of the practical kind, he entered the army and
served until the close of the war. Then he returned to
the State of Michigan and embarked in the lumber business. Remaining there until 1868, he removed to Knox
county, this State, and engaged extensively in the walnut
lumber business as a specialty. He is now one of the
most enterprising men of that county, having in less than
six years assisted in clearing the timber from a large tract
of very valuable land, and in bringing it under cultivation,
giving employment to hundreds of worthy men. He has
also aided materially to advance the prosperty of the town
of Sandborn, a flourishing little village on the Indianapolis and Vincennes Railroad, thirty miles this side of the
latter place. Although a life-long Democrat, when he
became a candidate, which was not at his own solicitation,
Republicans as well as Democrats rallied around his stand-

ard, at the polls, and sent him, in a " triumphal car of victory," to the Legislature to represent the county, and not
the Democracy merely. He lives in Sandborn.

THEOHPALUS CRUMPACKER,

REPRESENTATIVE FROM PORTER.

Was born in Redford county, Virginia, January 18, 1823,
of German parentage. When eight years of age, the son
came West with his parents to grow up, etc, and abided
for a season of seven years in Union county, in this State
They then removed to Laporte county, where they continued to reside until 1863. At that time Mr. Crumpacker,
having had a hard time of it in his hand to mouth struggle
with poverty, settled down to rural pursuits in Porter
county, where he has since lived, and to some purpose,
having surmounted the obstacles that thickly beset the
path of youth and early manhood. In 1872, without seeking political position he was elected to the Legislature,
and re-elected again last October, and on the Republican
ticket, the Democratic candidate for State Senator carrying the county by two hundred majority. He is and has
been a Republican since the inception of the movement
that resulted in its organization. Before that he was a
Whig. He resides at Valparaiso.

HIRAM DALE,

REPRESENTATIVE FROM WABASH

Was born of American parentage, at Warrensburg, Fayette
county, this State, July 30, 1826. His father was a promi-

nent citizen of his county, serving three years as Director of the Whitewater Valley Canal when the company was first organized, and two or three terms as County Commis-sioner. Hiram however, had but limited opportunities for an education. Yet, by his own exertion, he qualified him-self for teaching and taught ten or twelve terms during the winter months, farming through the summer season. He claims to have contributed his mite to the advancement of the material and moral interests of his community and county. Before the disorganization of the Whig and the organization of the Republican party, he belonged to the first named organization ; since then and now, to the latter. His postoffice address is Dora, Wabash county.

JAMES MILTON DARNELL,

REPRESENTATIVE FROM HOWARD,

Is a native of Kentucky. He was born in Jessamine county, June 28, 1817. His father was a native of Mary-land and his mother of North Carolinia. The elder Darnell, not recognizing the divine right of man to enslave his fellow-man, as was maintained by the supporters of the slave system of the South, removed to the free State of Indiana in the fall of 1821. The son was then but four years of age. He lived and worked on the farm with his father until he was twenty years old ; then he was per-mitted to provide for himself, and succeeded so well that in a few years he had secured a splendid education at Han-over College. He accumulated the means to acquire this education by teaching school in the winter, and working on a farm in the summer. Then he studied medicine in the office of Dr. Brown, of Connersville, now of Indianapolis. In 1842 he commenced the practice of medicine in Carroll county, and continued the same until 1864, when he removed to Kokomo and engaged in the drug business, at which place and in which business he is yet engaged. In politics he first professed the principles of the Whig party, and voted with that organization until 1848, when he espoused the principles of the Free Soil party, and voted for Van Buren for President. When the Republican party was organized he thought he properly belonged to that, and became a Republican in principle and practice, and he is still true to the party tenets. Twice he held the office of Councilman for the city of Kokomo, through the favor of men of all parties, and was elected Representative at the last election over a Democratic and Independent candidate.

ALEXANDER A. DAVISON,

REPRESENTATIVE FROM JACKSON,

Was born at Dupont Powder Mills, in the little State of Delaware, on the 28th of June, 1836. His parents were natives of, and were married in Ireland. They came across the salted sea and settled at Seymour in 1864. The son lived on a farm, and attended district school until of lawful age to take care of himself. Then he entered the State University, but did not complete a collegiate course, merely spending two sessions in the preparatory department. Having served as Clerk in the city of Seymour in 1865, and subsequently serving satisfactorily as Councilman, and eventually as Mayor, in 1868 Mr. Davison was elected Treasurer of the county of Jackson. In 1872 he was re-elected and served another term. He was nominated for the office he now holds without his consent, and was elected without opposition, and then he consented to serve. In the earlier part of his career, Mr. Davison taught school and was clerk in a dry goods store. Latterly he engaged in the hardware business, devoting a part of his time and talent to editing the Seymour Democrat, which newspaper he owns. He is a graceful and a logical writer. In politics he is, and always has been a Democrat, though he did not take hold of crow in 1872 with real relish. However he did dine upon the corvine biped on election morn of that year. As a Democrat to-day he is not in favor of inflating the currency, nor can he see Democracy through greenback glasses, He is a tried and true Democrat of the Jackson and Jeffersonian school, modernized. Above all, he is honest in his political professions, and practices what he preaches.

JOHN STEELE DAVIS,

REPRESENTATIVE FROM FLOYD,

Was born at Dayton, Ohio, November 14th, 1814, and coming to Indiana in 1836, located at New Albany, where he has since continued to reside. His father was at one time a captain in the Federal army. The son was educated at Dayton and Troy, Ohio, and read law and has practiced that profession since. He began his political career as a Whig; was a member of the electoral college on the ticket for General Taylor, and was a member of the last Whig convention that ever convened, representing his adopted State, at large. After the disintegration of that organization he espoused the Democratic cause. He has spent six sessions in Indianapolis as a member of the House and two sessions as a member of the Senate, serving the State as a Legislator for fourteen years in all. He has also served the city of New Albany as a Councilman, City Clerk and Attorney, and the Democracy of the State four years as a member of the Central Committee.

The gentleman from Floyd, is a man of magnificent mien and noble bearing. When he addresses the House all is attention, for he has something to say when he speaks. He is familiar with all the forms and details of Legislative proceedings and new members find it to their advantage to keep an eye set on the chair of the member from New Albany.

JAMES GLASGOW EDWARDS,

REPRESENTATIVE FROM PUTNAM,

Was born in Clayborne county, Tennessee, June 13, 1815. His parents were American born, of Irish descent. When a babe in arms James Glasgow accompanied his parents to the then territory of Missouri, and in consequence he had for the companion of his early youth the fiery, untamed papoose. When he was six years of age, his parents picked him up and took him back to old Tennessee, where he was educated in a log cabin. In 1831 he came to this State, and locating in Putnam county assisted in clearing the forest from the rich soil of that blue grass region of Indiana, and lent a helping hand toward rearing all the log cabins of his community. In those days "log rolling bees" were as fashionable as apple parings and corn huskings and quiltings have been since. He attended twenty-seven log rollings, to say nothing of house raisings, in one spring. So you see when it came to political log rolling, he proved himself to be no slouch of a hand at the business. So successful was he at the business, he rolled into office the first attempt. Besides he is not a stranger to mauling rails. He even entertains the opinion that if rail mauling made Lincoln President, then he should have been Vice President. Politically Mr. Edwards has always been a Democrat, and can now see no necessity for a change in political principles.

JAMES EMERSON,

JOINT REPRESENTATIVE FROM BENTON AND NEWTON,

Was born in Piqua county, Ohio, December 9, 1820. His parents were of American birth, but foreign lineage; on his father's side Irish, on his mother's side German. When James was but eight years of age his parents removed from Ohio to Indiana. When he had attained the age the law regards as responsible and amenable to it he settled in Benton county, where he has since resided. The only education he was able to acquire was in the common or district schools of the rural regions where he was reared, so he adopted the avocation of a farmer, and followed that occupation all his life except when in office through

7

the elective or appointive powers of country and county.
Twice he has held the position of Township Trustee, and
once that of Treasurer of Benton county. For several years
he served his country in the discharge of the arduous duties
of postmaster at Catalpa Grove. A Democrat, until
recently, he became liberalized and drifted into independence of party and was elected to the Legislature on the
Independent ticket. Aydelotte. Benton county is his
address.

EDWARD EVANS.

REPRESENTATIVE FROM LAPORTE.

Was born in Meigs county, Ohio, July 25, 1819. His
parents were natives of Maryland. In 1829 the elder
Evans removed to Indiana, and with his family settled in
Vermillion county, where they lived until 1832, when they
removed to Laporte county. The son followed farming
with his father in the summer, and attended such schools
as were accessible in those early days, in the winter. His
life, up to 1861, was that of a well-to-do, quiet farmer, and
in fact so continued until 1874, notwithstanding the fact
that he was elected Township Trustee in 1861, and served
in that capacity until 1866. But it was not until 1874 that
his life became lively. Then, being a candidate for Representative, he began to learn what a mean man he was—in
the eyes of his opponents. He had always been a Democrat, and had kept the faith and was fighting the fight
faithfully, and as the sequel showed successfully.

JAMES CALVERT FAVORITE,

REPRESENTATIVE FROM HUNTINGTON,

Is a native of the county of that name, having been born
there February 21, 1842. His parents were of American
birth, his father a Pennsylvanian and his mother an
Ohioan. The son was educated in the common schools of
his native county, and in the collegiate institute at
Marion in this State. Soon after the breaking out of
the war, he enlisted in Co. H 75th Indiana, and served
with his regiment during the rebellion, ably assisting to
dispel the delusion under which the nation had labored
since the Mexican war, that Indiana volunteers would not
fight. With the gallant 75th, this Favorite of the people
of Huntington participated prominently in the bloody and
disastrous battle of Chickamauga, and also in the bloody
but brilliant victory of Missionary Ridge, and then
marched in triumph with Sherman to the sea. Since
those historical days he has been engaged in teaching
school and farming alternately, earning an honest living
and living honestly. These two occupations he lays
aside for a season now, to serve the State in the Legislative halls. In the distant future he will dandle his grand-
children on his knee and tell them how, in his early manhood, he served his country and State. In politics he is
and has been from the beginning of the party organization a Republican. Post office address, Huntington.

MARK E. FORKNER,

REPRESENTATIVE FROM HENRY,

Is a native of Indiana. He was born in Henry county.
January 26. 1846, and is the youngest appearing member

of the House as he is one of the ablest in debate. His parents were residents of Indiana as early as 1819. The son was educated at Newcastle Academy. always standing at the head of his class, being both an apt and a studious scholar. Having concluded his course of study at the Academy he read law with Judge Mellett. He was admitted to the bar at the early age of twenty years, and for three years enjoyed the privilege of practicing, with Judge Millett for a partner.

MARTIN CALVIN FULK,

REPRESENTATIVE FROM GREENE,

Was born in Surrey county, North Carolina, March 15, 1823. His parents were German on his father's and Scotch on his mother's side. They were poor, and left North Carolina when the son was a mere child, for the free State of Indiana, though it was then a wilderness. They did this because they were determined that their children should not do as they had done, compete with slave labor in a poor country, for thus they had been kept in poverty. So in October, 1829, the Fulk family set out for the State of Indiana. They first stopped in Monroe county, and remained there a year and a half. Then they settled in Greene, where three or four years afterwards the wife and mother died, leaving the husband and seven children. The subject of this sketch was the oldest, and he had to help support the family from that time until he had arrived at the age of twenty-one. It was on this account that he did not receive the full benefit of even such very common schools as were then established in that unsettled section of the

State. When of age he began business for himself as a farmer, and followed that occupation until 1850, when he united with the Baptist Church and entered the ministry. Since then his time has been about equally divided between his plow and his pulpit.

In politics Mr. Fulk was a Democrat for the ten years preceding the war, though he exercised large discretion in voting for men and measures, always aiming to support such as would best advance morality. In 1861 he thought the truest interest of the country required his support of the Republican party in its struggle to maintain the union of the States. With that organization he acted through- out the war then inaugurated, and until its corruption drove him from it. recently. Not being able to see any hope of deliverance through the Democratic party he became independent in politics and favored the organiza- tion of a new party, one which would give the necessary relief. He was elected by the Independents of Greene. Parke postoffice is his address.

JOSEPH GILBERT,

REPRESENTATIVE FROM VIGO,

Was born at Terre Haute, January 2, 1839. His father, Curtis Gilbert, was a native of Connecticut, and coming to Indiana in early life, he located in Vigo county, becoming one of the pioneers of the State. He at once became thoroughly identified with the interests of Indiana in gen- eral and Terre Haute in particular. He was the first Clerk of the county, and served three terms of seven years each, in succession. For fourteen years, he was President of the Terre Haute Branch of the old Indiana State Bank. The son was born on a seven acre farm (though not with a silver spoon in his mouth), corner Sixth and Main streets, now near the very heart of the beautiful little city of Terre Haute. There he lived three years, and moved, with his parents, to what is now known as the Gilbert homestead, in the eastern environs of the city. He lived there until he had attained manhood's estate, having in the meantime acquired a good education at Wabash College, Crawfordsville. Then he began business for himself as an agriculturist and horticulturist, on his own farm, near the city, where he was born and reared. He has been identified with those interests ever since, and is now known and recognized throughout the State as a leader in all that tends to advance agriculture and horticulture. He has served as Secretary of the Terre Haute Horticultural Society seven years since its organization, ten years since, and also as Secretary of the Vigo Agricultural Society six out of the eight years of its existence. For two years he was Corresponding Secrectary of the Indiana State Horticultural Society, and at the last annual meeting, a few weeks since, at Plainfield, he was elected President of that organization.

In politics Mr. Gilbert is a Democrat of the more conservative class, and prominently identified with the Grange movement, which, while it is not a political organization for political purposes, is nevertheless an organization that has more or less political effect. Mr. Gilbert was initiated into the first Grange of Patrons of Husbandry organized in this State, which event transpired in his native county, in December, 1870. He is Master of the County Council there now. Mr. Gilbert is a temperance man, and will not vote for the repeal of the Baxter bill until he is assured that something better can be secured in its stead. For four years he was Chairman of the Vigo County Democratic Central Committee, and at the last election was chosen Representative by eight hundred and five majority, quite a number of Granger and temperance Republicans voting for him. Withal, the State can not have too many citizens of the character of the gentleman from Vigo.

EUGENIUS B. GLASGOW,

REPRESENTATIVE FROM STEUBEN,

Was born in Wayne county, Ohio, January 28th, 1834. His parents were of Scotch, German and Welsh descent. The son was reared on his father's farm. In the summer he worked, and in the winter, attended school as boys now do in the country. At the age of twenty, however, he attended Oberlin College, in Ohio, and afterwards taught school a while, studying law in the meantime. In 1859, he removed to Illinois, and in 1860, was admitted to the bar at Mount Vernon, that State, in 1861 he removed to Benton county, this State, and in 1863, he enlisted in the army, and was assigned to duty in the 128th Indiana Infantry, where he served until the close of the war. Then he settled down to the practice of law in Angola, where he now resides and practices his profession. He was elected to the Legislature from Steuben in 1872, and served through his term so satisfactorily to his constituents that he was re-elected last fall for another term. He is now, what he has been since the organization of the party —a Republican.

ANDREW JACKSON GOSSMAN,

REPRESENTATIVE FROM MARTIN AND DUBOIS,

Was born on the Atlantic ocean, between Bremen and Baltimore, on the 19th of October, 1830. His parents were Germans from Bavaria. He came to Indiana in 1853, and although formerly a miller by trade is a farmer at present. After arriving in this State, Mr. Gossman lived in Wayne, and afterward in Henry county. In December, 1855, he married, and in 1863 removed to Dubois county. Here he bought a farm of 180 acres, where he is still living. After keeping store for five years, he resumed rural pursuits. in which he is still engaged. Mr. Gossman has always been a Democrat. His parents were able to give him only about six months' attendance at a district school. He held the office of Justice of the Peace nearly five years. His residence is in Dubois county, and his postoffice address Jasper.

SAMUEL HARPER,

REPRESENTATIVE FROM LAGRANGE,

Was born in Ireland in the merry month of May, 1824. His parents were Irish and Scotch. In early life he saluted the Blarney Stone and started for the new world on a voyage of discovery. He traveled in Canada, Ohio, and Michigan, staying in the latter State long enough to receive a classical education at the State University. In 1850 he discovered Indiana, and liking the State he settled therein. He has been living in Lagrange county ever since, as near as the writer is able to ascertain. He is, and has been a farmer during all that time, and hitherto has held no office but that of Township Trustee for Greenfield township, his adopted county, from 1872 to 1874. He has preferred the quiet walks of private to the turbulent boulevards of public life. Before the fall of the institution of slavery in the South, he was an avowed Abolitionist, but is now a Republican. He lives near Orland.

GEORGE W. HARRIS.

REPRESENTATIVE FROM MADISON.

Was born in Ross county, Ohio, on the 4th of July, 1822. His father and mother were natives of Augusta county, Virginia, the former of English, the latter of Irish descent. They came to this State and settled in Henry county in 1833, but for the last thirty-three years, have resided in Madison county. Representative Harris was reared a farmer, never graduated from any school, and never held any office until elected to the one he now holds. But he has exalted ideas of honesty. and fixedness of purpose, and while he may not electrify his fellow members and the country with unchained eloquence, he can always be relied upon to record his vote for the right. His address is Anderson, Madison county.

BRANSON L. HARRIS.

REPRESENTATIVE FROM WAYNE.

Was born in Green Township, Wayne county, Indiana April 21st, 1817. His parents were natives of North Carolina. They removed to the State in 1811, when it was an Indian Territory. In 1812 the elder Harris enlisted in the Federal army, and served in the war with England, which was then inaugurated. When that "cruel war was over," he returned to Indiana and settled in Wayne Township, where for many years he was a Justice of the Peace. He was educated in the common schools, such as were then accessible. He followed farming for a livelihood, as did his father before him. But Cincinnatus-like, he was taken from the plow and carried on the shoulders of the populace, as it were, into the halls of State, twenty-two years ago, where he served one session in the Lower House. Politically he was a Clay Whig so long as there were any. Since then and now, a Republican. Greenfork postoffice is his address.

BENJAMIN F. HAVENS.

REPRESENTATIVE FROM VIGO,

Was born in Burlington, Rush county, this State, July 24, 1839. He descended from the older families of Virginia on the one side, and Connecticut on the other; but his parents direct came to Indiana from Kentucky and Ohio. His grandfather, Havens, was the Peter Cartwright of Indiana Methodism about a half century ago, and his name was a household word in every well-regulated family of that faith for many years after he had passed to the reward of the righteous.

The father of the subject of this sketch was a mechanic and was only able to give the son the benefit of one year at Asbury University. So at the age of nineteen years. Mr. Havens was thrown upon his own resources for the acquirement of the collegiate education he coveted. But he was equal to the emergency. By close application. teaching school and studying alternately. he was able to finish up his education at the State University. He then read law and became quite proficient in the profession. For two years he was City Attorney of Terre Haute and discharged the duties of the trust with distinguished ability throughout his term of service.

Politically Mr. Havens is a Democrat. of firm convictions, as to the correctness of his principles. In this respect he does not follow in the footsteps of his fathers, for he is the first and only Democrat of the family, He learned his Democracy in the school of Willard, Robinson and Hendricks, and like them he will never falter in the faith. Personally, the gentleman from Vigo is very popular and universally commands the attention of an often listless House, when he arises to address the Assembly upon matters of moment to the State.

JOHN HENRY HAYNES.

REPRESENTATIVE FROM PERRY,

Was born in Breckenridge county. Kentucky, August 15, 1832. His father was born in Virginia; his

mother was a native of Kentucky. He received a common
school education in his native State and emigrated to Indiana in 1857; he then studied medicine, graduating from
the medical department of the University of Louisville.
He settled down to the practice of his profession in
Spencer county and subsequently in Perry county, where
he has since resided. During the war, however, he served
his country as Captain of what was known as the Clarke
Township Company, Indiana Legion—the 5th regiment—
from 1862 to 1864.

Politically. Mr. Haynes was a Whig, voting for Bell and
Everett in 1860. Now and since then he has been a Democrat, and was elected to the Legislature on the Democratic ticket. Address the gentleman from Perry at
Adyeville.

JOHN D. HIGHWAY,

REPRESENTATIVE FROM KOSCIUSKO.

Was born in Warner county, Ohio, December 15th, 1811.
His parents were American born, of English extraction,
and his father was for many years a Justice of the Peace
in his native State. In 1834 the son was married to Miss
Sarah Antram, also of Warren county, State of Ohio. In
1843 they removed to Indiana, and located in Kosciusko
county, and to date have reared a promising family of six
children besides helping to level the primitive forest, and
otherwise, bring order out of the original chaos of their
adopted county. Since 1856 Mr. Highway has almost
constantly served his county as Commissioner, and in that

capacity he has had many highways beside his own to
care for. So well did he discharge all the trusts committed
to his care, that his county concluded to send him to the
Legislature last fall. Like so many of our legislators,
he was a Whig in early life, but, unlike the majority
of them this session, he is a Republican now. Beseige
him with letters in his stronghold at Sevastapol.

MAHLON HELLER,

REPRESENTATIVE FROM ALLEN,

Is a native of Pennsylvania. He was born at Bushkill,
Pike county, February 24, 1831. His parents were of Ger-
man descent but American birth. His father was a promi-
nent citizen of the noble old Key Stone Commonwealth.
For five years he was Associate Judge of the Pike County
Court, and for two years he was treasurer of the county.
Besides, he was a justice of the peace for thirty years.
Representative Heller was educated in the common schools
and the more practical school of active business life, both
public and private. He is emphatically a self-made man.
He was auditor of his native county two terms. In 1868,
he removed to Indiana and settled in Allen county, where
he at once commanded attention and favor. In 1872, he
was elected to the Legislature, and served with distinction
through the session of 1872–3. He is now one of the most
active members of the House. There is not a man in that
body better versed in the routine of legislative proceedings. He is ever on the alert for the tricks of the opposition to smuggle some odious measure of legislation through.

The democracy of Allen county and the State may well put their trust in him, for he will watch their interests with ceaseless vigil, and advocate their cause ably and eloquently. If there is a true Democrat in the House, the gentleman from Allen is the man. Monroeville is his post office address.

MORTIMER L. HENDERSON,

REPRESENTATIVE FROM RIPLEY,

Was born in Ripley county, this State, November 1st, 1830, of Virginia and Kentucky parentage. He was educated in the district school, near the farm of his father, on which he was reared, and in Moro Hill College, but when not traveling, he has followed farming for a living In 1852 he crossed the Plains for the benefit of his health, being then affected with the yellow or gold fever. Two years effected a permanent cure, and he returned healthy and happy in 1858. Once in his life he was clerk on a steamboat which ploughed the waves of the Ohio and the Cumberland. He has traveled too much to be caught napping. In politics he had been identified with the Democratic party all his life until just before the last election, when he refused to act with the old time honored organization any longer on account of local corruptions. In his own language, he "bolted the Democratic county convention in consequence of local corruptions, was taken up by the Independents, and by them nominated for Representative, but was elected by both parties over his opponent, Frank Alexander, a lawyer."

JAMES HOPKINS,

REPRESENTATIVE FROM MARION,

Was born a Yankee, on Sourthern soil, in the halcyon days of human slavery. In other words, the subject of this sketch was ushered into life at Newport, Kentucky, June 15, 1815, and his parents were natives of Yankee land, his father of Massachusetts and his mother of Connecticut. For ten years, immediately following the incorporation of Covington, the elder Hopkins was President of the City Council. The son was the eldest of eleven children, and at a tender age was regarded as the second staff of support for the family. His father was a brick moulder, and he moulded his first progeny into a brick maker. During the winter, when the brick yards could not be operated, he was allowed to attend school if one was within reach, and tuition was not too altitudinous for the paternal purse. At the lawful age of twenty he left the parental protection, and stalked out upon the stage of life for himself. Thinking he would like brick-laying better than making, he applied for an apprenticeship, was engaged, and in three years had learned the trade. After following it for two years, he married a most estimable Christian lady, with whom he lived in harmony for thirty years, rearing six out of nine children born to them, whom they educated to be useful members of the community, both business and social. In his life Mr. Hopkins has himself been an exemplary member of the Methodist Church. He has lived in the South, at Greencastle, and now in this city. Thrice he has amassed a competency of the world's wealth and thrice has he lost all, the last time by the Greencastle fire, and a short time before, the greatest loss of his life—his wife.

Now, at the advanced age of 55, with a clear record and a clear conscience, he begins the battle of life anew. Politically he was a Clay Whig during the life of the great statesman, a Union man during the war, and now an opponent of the Administration and a Trades Unionist of the deepest dye. He claims that through the unions and through no other agency can the laboring masses of the country find relief from the oppression by which they are environed. He is also an avowed temperance man from principle.

PATRICK HORN,

REPRESENTATIVE FROM ALLEN,

First knew this life on March 16, 1819, in Kings county, Ireland. His parents were of Scottish and Irish descent, and died when he was yet young. Young Horn inherited a small estate, the sale of which enabled him to emigrate to this country, landing in New York City in 1830. He soon apprenticed himself to a baker, and followed that business until his removal to Fort Wayne in 1837. At this time Fort Wayne was only a small town, and Mr. Horn bought a small farm, and commenced immediately its improvement. In 1845 he married a daughter of Robert Baird, Esq., and the twain lived "as one flesh" a happy life until 1873, when the wife died. Representative Horn received his education in Ireland, and in Fort Wayne, it being necessarily rudimentary. He has held the office of Town Trustee and Township Assessor. This gentleman has always been a Democrat, and never has been false to the principles of the party. He lives at Huntertown.

EDWARD TONY JACKSON,

REPRESENTATIVE FROM VERMILLION,

Was born in Clearmont county, Ohio, July 29, 1807. His father was of Irish and his mother of German descent. His opportunities for schooling were confined to a house without a shingle roof, a glass window or a plank floor. Fitted by education for farming, he adopted that avocation. Since 1830 he has resided in Vermillion county and held all the offices within the gift of the citizens of that county, except constable, and to that he did not aspire; and yet he never sought office; "waiting for the wagon," as he would express it. Always opposed to corruption, he had to abandon the Republican party sometime since, and now he is independent in politics. His home is near Hilsdale.

JAMES LEWIS JOHNSON,

REPRESENTATIVE FROM CARROLL,

Was born in Carroll county, July 4, 1849. His parents were natives of Virginia, but of Irish and Scotch ancestry. He came to this State in 1834. Mrs. Johnson died while he the subject of this sketch was too young to know of the inestimable boon of a mother's living presence. His father, however, is a wealthy farmer, and gave him the advantages of a good education, at Asbury University. For the last six or seven years, he has taught school, more or less, and regards that as his profession. He was known at college, and is now known in Carroll county, as an able debater, and he will probably make his mark during the session. He has always been a Democrat, and acts uniformly with that party.

8

COLUMBUS JOHNSTON,

REPRESENTATIVE FROM DEARBORN,

Was born in Manchester township, Dearborn county, Indiana, January 7, 1832. His parents were both American, his father from Virginia and his mother from Kentucky, they coming to this State as early as 1811. The son was reared in his father's mill, and only had such school accommodations as the common or district school afforded. When he had made the most of them, he settled down to the business he had followed for his father, in his own interest. He is one of the honest hard working members of the House. Early in the session he was appointed one of a committee of three to investigate the affairs of the Ohio and Mississippi road, and to ascertain if the company was complying with the conditions of its charter. Being of an investigating turn of mind and a man of unflinching integrity, he may be said to be the right man in the right place. In politics he is a staunch Democrat. Johnston's Mills is his post office address.

ELIJAH T. KEIGHTLY,

JOINT REPRESENTATIVE FROM MARION AND SHELBY,

Was born in Oldham county, Kentucky, July 7, 1833, of American parentage. He came to Indiana July 18, 1849, at the age of sixteen, having first received an education thus early in life at Funk's Masonic College, Lagrange, Kentucky. Next he located at Franklin, then at Noblesville, and subsequently in Greencastle, and was elected

Auditor of Putnam county for four years in 1862. He moved to Indianapolis soon after his term of service had expired. Last fall he was elected to the Legislature by an aggregate majority of 2,019, receiving 1,356 of that majority in Marion and the balance in Shelby. In politics Mr. Keightly is a Democrat of the old school, having held the proud position of Postmaster under President Jackson, in the halcyon days of honest government, home rule, hard money, and sound sense generally. To be an office-holder in those days was not to be subservient to the whims and caprices of any man or set of men on the ground of party expediency or necessity. The gentleman from Marion and Shelby resides in Indianapolis.

EVENDER CHALANE KENNEDY,

REPRESENTATIVE FROM MARION,

Was born in Muncie, Delaware county, February 14, 1842. His parents were from the classical town known to fame as Killarney, in the county of Kerry, situated in the beautiful Emerald Isle, by the deep sounding sea; but they came to this State in 1831. Thus it happened that Evender had the honor of a Hoosier birthright. His father, Hon. Andrew Kennedy, was for four years a member of the General Assembly of this State, and six years a Member of Congress from the 5th and 10th Districts, respectively. With all he was a well known Indiana politician. The son was educated at Asbury, and after a thorough course of reading and study of law, he entered upon the practice of his profession. Hardly had he time

to consult a client when grim visaged war stalked forth in
the land, and aroused the martial spirit within him. He
enlisted early and entered active service speedily. During
the sharp and decisive struggle that ensued he rose from
the ranks to staff service, with commission as a Captain.
It is needless to add that he made a rattling record in the
service. At the close of the war he went to Kansas, and
was elected to the Legislature. The experience he received
in legislative work there he brings to the discharge of his
duties here. Politically he is a Democrat, and descended
from a race born and cradled in the faith for four genera-
tions. Mr. Kennedy has also made quite a literary record,
being the author of the epic poems, "Osseo" and "Code of
Blood," besides others, and numerous prose productions,
romantic and rollicking in their character. Though yet
a young man, his life has been an eventful and a spirited
one. He lives in the thirteenth ward, in the city of Indianapolis.

PETER S. KENNEDY,

REPRESENTATIVE FROM MONTGOMERY,

Was born in Bourbon county, Kentucky, July 10th, 1829,
of Irish, Dutch and Welsh descent. He came to this State
in 1853; resided first at Danville until 1865, then he removed
to Crawfordsville, where he now lives in luxurous ease, in
the suburbs of the city. He began business in life as a
blacksmith, but through his own exertions he acquired a
good education, and attained eminence in the practice of
the profession of law. In 1856 he was elected Prosecuting

Attorney of the Indianapolis Circuit, and proved a terror to evil doers in the district bounded by his official limits. Though he has never befoie been in the Legislature, he has influenced Legislation in a large degree. His friends claim that he is the real author of the law, permitting criminals to testify in their own behalf, and giving the prosecution the closing speech in the case; and also the law revising the judicial system of this State, besides several others, in the interest of the public. Before 1856, he was a Whig in politics, but a rank Anti-Slavery advocate. Since then he has been a Republican, seeing the evils of the Slavery system in the South. He was an Abolitionist from his earliest boyhood. He is an able advocate of the temperance reform and leads his party in the House generally.

JOHN KENNEDY,

REPRESENTATIVE FROM MORGAN,

Was born in Lamb's Bottom, that county, September 30, 1833. His father was of Irish descent, though born in Kentucky; his mother of German descent, but a native of Kentucky. Both reside in Morgan county, where they settled when they first came to the State in 1830.

Representative Kennedy received his education through private teaching at his home, though he took a partial course at Bellville Academy in Hendricks county, and also at the Edinburg Grammar School, securing an engagement as assistant teacher in the latter institution in 1855.

During intermissions he read medicine under the tutelage of Dr. Clarke, of Edinburg. In the spring of

1856, his health having failed, he returned to the farm, where he soon regained his health, and then soon afterward engaged in teaching a school in Sangamon county, Illinois, near Springfield. During the time he taught there he devoted spare hours to the acquirement of his chosen profession. Returning to Indiana in the spring of 1858, he spent the summer in the study of medicine under the instruction of Dr. Osgood, of Gosport. That winter he attended lectures at the Eclectic Medical Institute, Cincinnati. When he had completed his course he engaged in the practice of his profession within three miles of the old homestead, where he still resides, taking rank among the wealthiest citizens of the county. It is said that as a member of the Christian church, a worker in the Sunday school cause, and a leader in good works, Dr. Kennedy has exerted a benign influence wherever he has been, especially in Morgan county. Politically he is a Republican.

JAMES WARREN LANHAM,

REPRESENTATIVE FROM JEFFERSON,

Was born in Milton township, that county, January 31st, 1832. Both his parents and all his grand parents, were born on American soil, but his remote ancestors represented four nationalities, viz : English, Welsh, Irish and German. With the exception of two brief intervals, his home has always been in his native county. He was educated in Hanover College, and then taught school for a number of years, subsequently becoming a disciple of

Christ and a member of His ministry, in the Christian Church. Of late years, however, owing to a throat affection, and an over weening desire to serve the State, perhaps, he has not devoted himself so assiduously to ministerial dutes as in the earlier days of his ministrations. He has not sought, as some, to introduce politics into religion, but to infuse the spirit of religion into politics.

In politics he has been a Republican since the candidacy of Fremont, voting for the Rocky Mountain explorer in 1856, when he did not expect another man in the township to do so. When the votes were counted, his surprise to see twelve votes counted out for Fremont, can be better imagined than described. He is not the kind of a politician to deny his principles when his party is in the minority. He is an unflinching advocate of temperance, and an avowed champion of the local option feature of that great reform, and advocates a license for the school fund as well. He is also an open advocate of economy and education, and in short, of all State and national mental and moral advancement. Mr. Lanham makes his home at Moreville.

LEWIS C. LAW,

JOINT REPRESENTATIVE FROM SCOTT, JENNINGS AND
JEFFERSON,

Was born in Graham township, Jefferson county, Indiana, February 14, 1838. His parents were native born. He spent all but the last four years of his life in his native county. Until he was of age he worked on his father's farm in summer and attended the district school in winter;

and as his father's family was not of the office holding kind, little did he dream, as the country pedagogue applied the limp twig to train the youthful spine, that he would ever represent three such counties as Jefferson, Jennings and Scott in the halls of State at the city of concentric circles. But such is the history of current events, and so let it be recorded. Mr. Law has been a Democrat at all times, in all places, under all circumstances, and he is not ashamed of it. He has to take his mail at Graham post-office of a Grant Postmaster, however, which humiliation he hopes to do away with after 1876.

DAVID ROHRER LEEPER.

REPRESENTATIVE FROM ST. JOSEPH,

Was born in St. Joseph county January 12, 1832. His father, Samuel, is of English descent, and was born in Washington county, Pennsylvania. His mother, now deceased, was of German extraction, and was born in Montgomery county, Ohio. The father, an energetic, successful farmer, now lives in the enterprising city of South Bend, where the subject of this sketch also resides, and near which place he owns and carries on a farm. When seventeen years old, Mr. Leeper got the California fever, and among the earliest pioneers crossed the plains, with an ox team, to the Pacific Slope, where, engaged in mining and lumbering, he remained until 1854, when he returned via of the Isthmus, to his native home. He then attended school two years, in his county, at the Mishawaka Institute, (taught by Prof. Bellows, now of Ann Arbor University)' where, with his former schooling, he acquired a tolerably fair English education. Montana Territory found him a citizen of her borders from 1864 to 1868. He was here engaged with twenty-five to thirty heavy teams, in freighting and in logging in the lumber woods.

Originally a Whig and Republican, Mr. Leeper now battles under the Liberal banner. His parents have never sat in official chairs, and the present Representative now, for the first time, sits in Legislative halls. Two years ago he was nominated by the Liberals and Democrats for Representative, but declined on account of his business relations. Again, last fall, he was nominated and elected by the same political elements, being the first Representative ever elected in the county in opposition to the Whig or Republican party. The Democrats, having no candidate of their own, generally supported Mr. Leeper, his opponent being the regular Republican nominee. The gentleman from St. Joseph is afflicted somewhat with a weakness for the quill, and, for the past fifteen or twenty years, has occasionally contributed to the local newspapers political articles, editorials, and letters of travel written while on his frequent pleasure rambles in various parts of the country.

JOHN CRAWFORD LINCOLN,

REPRESENTATIVE FROM WARREN,

Was born in Preble county, Ohio, November 20, 1819. His parents were English. When John Crawford was but ten years of age, his parents removed to this State. That was before Indiana had attained the celebrity of having the best common school system and the largest school fund of any State in the Union, and in fact long before she enjoyed that proud distinction by right. Therefore the subject of this sketch was able to acquire but a limited education. Since his sparse school days, he has been a farmer in Warren county. By favor of the Republicans, to which party he belonged until recently, he has held the office of Trustee of township and county most of the time since 1863, though but one at a time, of course. He is now an Independent, and was elected to the Legislature on that ticket West Lebanon is where he lives.

JOHN S. MARTIN,

REPRESENTATIVE FROM FRANKLIN,

Was born in Brookville, November 24, 1835. His parents were of the old pioneers of Franklin county, having removed there early in life, from the Carolinas. With such surroundings, the son had but poor opportunities for securing even the semblance of a common school education. But he became an active student in the great school of practical life, a training that the collegiates of the present day lack. When his few school days, so far as books were concerned, had concluded, he did not, Macawber-like, and like the young men of this degenerate day, wait for something to turn up, but proceeded at once to turn something up. He engaged in farming and turned up the soil of his native county, and he has been engaged in that pursuit, with the purpose of making an honest living by the sweat of his brow, for seven years. He lives now where he has lived since his birth. His constituents, recognizing his honesty and integrity in private life, concluded last fall to call him into public prominence; so they elected him to the Legislature. He is and was always a Democrat.

AUGUSTUS NEWTON MARTIN,

JOINT REPRESENTATIVE FROM ADAMS AND WELLS.

Was born at Whitestown, Butler county, Pennsylvania, March 23, 1847. His parents were of American birth and Irish descent. His father was Auditor of Butler county, Pennsylvania, three years. Mr. Martin was educated at Witherspoon Institute, in his native county, and at Eastman's Commercial College, Poughkeepsie, N. Y. In the earlier part of the war he enlisted in the 58th Regiment, Pennsylvania volunteers, and participated in the cheerful chase after John Morgan through the border States, and assisted in his capture in Ohio. He was then but 16 years of age. Soon afterwards, he entered the 78th Regiment Pennsylvania Volunteer Infantry, and served therein until discharged for disability from disease, in August, 1865. In 1869 he came to Indiana and located at Bluffton, where he begun the practice of the law in 1870, and he now has a large practice and a large acquaintance throughout the section of the State where he lives. Considering the vicissitudes in life with which Mr. Martin has had to contend, he is far advanced on the high road to prosperity. He was born a Democrat and never knew a change in political faith.

HENRY M. MARVIN,

REPRESENTATIVE FROM BOONE,

Was born in Putnam county, New York, November 6, 1821. His father was of English extraction, and his mother of German descent. He was educated in the common schools of New York, and at Vermilyea Academy, in Carmels. New York State. At the age of nineteen, he was released from the paternal apron strings, and slid out for New York city, to see the sights of that mighty metropolis. In two years he saw all the sights he cared to see there, and after a close communion with the columns of the Tribune, he concluded to come West. And it came to pass that in 1843 he was at the opening of the White Water Valley Canal, at Connersville. There he heard the first speeches, to which he listened in this State. The first was from Governor Biggler, a Whig, and he was followed by Governor Whitcomb, a Democrat, who was elected in 1843, the same year the Democrats first came into power in Indiana. Their motto then was retrenchment and reform, and Mr. Marvin says that is the watchword now, and if the party does not live up to it, it will have its reward. He claims that he was educated an old-fashioned Whig, but is a square-toed Democrat now. He represented Boone in the Legislature from 1850 to 1856. and has held many county offices, in which county he has lived since 1843. His address is Northfield.

JESSIE MARVIN,

REPRESENTATIVE FROM FOUNTAIN,

Is a native of Mason county, Kentucky, where he was born May 17, 1807. His parents were of American birth and English extraction. They died when the son was not yet able to take care of himself on account of his extreme youth. For years afterwards he was buffeted about by the hard hand of fortune. All the education he was able to acquire was of that practical character that comes alone through the experience of the self-made man of the times. Mr. Marvin was always blessed with good health and amply able to care for his physical necessities. By dint of perseverence in labor and economy he has accumulated considerable property. Knowing how hard it is to earn money, he is not inclined to expend it lavishly. He is a firm believer in the principles that public business should be transacted on the bases of private business as to expenditures. His vote will be recorded accordingly upon all appropriations. While Mr. Marvin may not make many speeches during the session, he can be relied upon for some substantial voting. Attica is his postoffice address, and he is a Democrat.

JOHN L. MEGINITY,

JOINT REPRESENTATIVE FROM ORANGE AND CRAWFORD,

Was born in Henry county, Kentucky, July 31, 1833. His father was of Irish and his mother of French descent. Having received a good common school education, he taught school in the counties of Henry, Oldham, and

Trimble, in the State of Kentucky. In the meantime he read law. In 1861 he removed to Orange county, this State, and had been in the State but two or three years when he was elected surveyor of his adopted county. In 1864 he was elected to the office of Clerk of the Circuit Court, and in 1868 was appointed to fill a vacancy. In one way and another he continued to hold that office until October, 1874.

Since his removal to this State, when not engaged in the discharge of the duties of office, he has practiced the profession of law. He has been a Democrat all his life and he is so still. Paoli is his postoffice address.

JOHN R. MILLER,

JOINT REPRESENTATIVE FROM PARKE AND MONTGOMERY,

Is a native of the first-named county. He was born in Raccoon township, February 10, 1825. He traces his lineage back to Germany and Ireland, though his parents were American born. They were among the earliest pioneers, of Parke county, and the Miller family is known all through Western Indiana and Eastern Illinois, and universally respected. The elder Miller was a resident of Parke county for more than a half century, and did not die until some three years since. In his life time he was Justice of the Peace fifteen years, County Commissioner eight years, Township Trustee several years, and always a Democrat. General Jackson was his patron saint, politically, and when Old Hickory died there was not one left to take his place. Mrs. Miller, the mother of John R., is still living on the old homestead and she has lived in Parke county longer than any other person now living in it. The subject of this sketch was educated in the common schools of his native county and at Asbury University. He has always been a farmer, and now lives on the oldest settled farm in Parke county. The first and second houses ever built in Parke county were built on that same farm, the first in the spring and the second in the fall of 1816. Mr. Miller, was elected Treasurer of his native county in 1855, and so satisfactorily did he serve he was re-elected for the second term. In politics he, like his father, always was a Democrat. He avows himself now as not being in favor of returning to specie payments while such an enormous indebtedness is hanging over the American people, especially since that indebtedness was incurred under a great greenback inflation. But he is in favor of a paper money issued directly to the people by the government, based on the faith and resources of the nation, to be made a full legal tender in the payment of all debts within the United States, both public and private (except such as were, by the laws or contracts originally creating them, made payable otherwise); the volume of such currency to be made adjustable to the business wants of the country. He inclines to the opinion that to make it interchangeable with government bonds, at an equitable rate of interest, at the option of the holder, will determine the needed volume. As will be observed, Mr. Miller has a Plan, to which the writer would invoke the attention of Jefferson and Jackson, if they can materialize. The address of the gentleman from Parke and Montgomery is Bridgeton, Parke county.

WILLIAM H. MILLER,

REPRESENTATIVE FROM VANDERBURGH,

Was born in Montgomery county, Ohio, of American ancestors, November 20, 1824. William only received a common school education, and so he concluded that he had best learn a trade, and selecting that of machinist, he applied himself closely and soon acquired a thorough knowledge of the business. During the war he served in the 24th Ohio Infantry, and was wounded three times, first at Green River in the side, second at Pittsburg Landing or Shiloh in the right arm, and third at Chickamauga, in the left arm. In 1864 he first came to this State, and in 1871 stopped for a season in Indianapolis, going to Evansville the same year. There he has been ever since engaged at his trade. Last fall, the Republicans, with whom he had voted previously, and the Independents, who had confidence in him, agreed among themselves to elect him their Representative, and they did. Though nominated without his knowledge and consent, Mr. Miller was elected by that coalition.

JACOB WARWICK MONTGOMERY,

REPRESENTATIVE FROM GIBSON,

Was born on the banks of Black river, February 11, 1811, within a mile and a half of where he now lives. His parents were prominent pioneers in that part of the great State of Indiana. His father had come from Virginia and his mother from South Carolina. Those were the days of hard work and poor schools, and he got more than his share of the former and less than his share of the latter. He did not even graduate from the old log school house. Having helped to clear a tract of land, it was luxury and ease to live the life of a farmer thereon, afterwards. So the subject of this sketch has always been a farmer, though of late years he has made a specialty of stock dealing. He was born and bred a Democrat, and was one of the faithful few during fourteen years of disaster and defeat, and now that the faith of his fathers has reasserted itself he can stand it still. True to party in times that tried the true Democratic soul, when the time of success had again arrived, it was fit and proper that Mr. Montgomery should be selected to represent the Democracy of Gibson in the halls of State. He was so selected. Owensville, Gibson county, is his address.

JAMES WESLEY MORGAN,

REPRESENTATIVE FROM HENDRICKS,

Was born in West Virginia, December 23, 1831, of American parentage. The same year of his birth his parents removed to Indiana, and located at Danville, in Hendricks county, where the subject of this sketch has always lived, thoroughly identifying himself with the interests of the county. Trained a farmer, Representative Morgan has since followed that occupation, dealing largely in stock. He was educated in the common schools of that county. He professes and practices the political faith of the Republican party, and was elected under the auspices of the managers of that party in Hendricks county. Mr.

9

Morgan is an energetic member and would be mistaken
for a professional man when participating in legislative
proceedings.

SMITH McCORD,

REPRESENTATIVE FROM HANCOCK,

Was born in Clearmont county, Ohio, November 12, 1819.
Both his parents, though American by birth, were of Irish
descent. He was educated in the common schools of Ohio
and Indiana, removing to this State with his parents in
1831. Like other young men of the olden time he attended
the district school in the winter and worked on his father's
farm in the summer. When he had attained the age of
maturity he engaged in farming for himself. Before his
election to the Legislature he had never held any office
except that of Justice of the Peace, which he has held
since 1860. He professes the political principles of
Democracy and his practice conforms thereto. His postoffice address is McCordsville, in his adopted county, that
town having been named in honor of the McCords.

CORNELIUS McFADDEN,

REPRESENTATIVE FROM JOHNSON,

Was born of American parentage, in Boone county, Ohio,
January 8th, 1832, and was educated in the common
schools of that county and State. Having attained his
majority in 1853, he left Ohio and came West to Indiana,

where he has since been busily engaged in growing up
with the country and with average success. He located,
upon his arrival, in Johnson county, and lives there still.
Farming is, and has always been his occupation. He was
a Democrat until he could see no hope of relief from the
administration of the party in power, through the old-time
honored party of the past. He has been independent in
politics of late years. and favored the organization of a
new party on new issues. The majority of the people of
Johnson, it seems, were of the same way of thinking, for
they sent him to the Legislature on the Independent ticket.
He lives at Trafalgar.

WILLIAM C. McMICHAEL,

REPRESENTATIVE FROM ST. JOSEPH AND MARSHALL,

Was born in Harris township, St. Joseph county, this State,
April 27, 1841. His parents were pioneers of American
nativity. The son had a hard row to hoe in early life,
being the eldest of thirteen children. In his boyhood he
had to work on his father's farm. In 1855 he discharged
the duties pertaining to the position of devil in the print-
ing office of the Mishawaka *Free Press*, with such skill
and fidelity as won for him the confidence and kindly consideration of his employer, and he was privileged to attend
school during the winter months of the year, which he did
for four seasons in succession. In this way he got a start
in literary life. Never neglecting an opportunity for study
he succeeded so well in the acquirement of knowledge
that he had the honor, in 1873, of having conferred upon
him the degree of Bachelor of Laws, by Notre Dame

University, at South Bend. He has never held any office before the one he holds now, is, and always has been, a Democrat. Present postoffice address, Mishawaka.

JAMES L. NASH,

REPRESENTATIVE FROM SULLIVAN,

Was born in Sullivan county, March 16, 1829. His parents were of Welsh descent, but American birth. The son was educated at Carlysle, in his native county and at home. There he engaged in the avocation of his father—agriculture. He has now one of the finest farms in Indiana, and is President of the Agricultural Society of Sullivan. It is said of him that ever since he stepped upon the stage of action, he has been an ardent and an active worker for the good of the community in which he lives, his efforts being the elevation of the standard of education, morality and religion. He has kept pace with the car of progress, and to-day holds a royal position among the workers and encouragers of education. He has had for his watchword, "higher, still higher;" and he has so successfully managed his public career, that not a blot or stain can be found upon his public record. Yet Mr. Nash has held official position for nearly a decade. He is and always was a Democrat, and time and again has he helped roll up the mighty majorities for Democracy that invariably come from old Sullivan county, rendering her a joy forever in the memory of the tried and true. The address of the gentleman from Sullivan, is Paxton.

ALBERT OSBORNE,

REPRESENTATIVE FROM ELKHART.

Is a native of New York. He was born in Otesgo county, in 1824, of German and English ancestry. His father was a minister in the Methodist Church. In 1835 the family removed to Michigan, where the son was educated in the common schools. He remained in that State until 1863, when he came to Indiana. Since then he has been a resident of this State, and engaged in agricultural pursuits. Politically he was first a Democrat, then a Republican, and now a Democrat. He remained a Republican until 1872, when he became Liberalised, supporting Mr. Greeley for the Presidency. He was the Liberal and Democratic nominee for the position he now holds in 1872, but was defeated by the stay at home vote, though the majority against him was not large. Being again nominated for that position at the last election, he was sent here by the votes of men of all parties, though he was most strenneously supported by Independents and Republicans. Goshen is his address.

WILLIAM T. PATE,

JOINT REPRESENTATIVE FROM SWITZERLAND AND OHIO,

Was born in Dearborn county, of American parentage, April 17, 1815. His early education, such as he was able to secure, was acquired at the old log school house on Saugheny Creek. When he had graduated, Mr. Pate engaged in agricultural pursuits, and also in the distilling business, and yet follows those avocations. For four years, however, he was Sheriff of Ohio county. During the war he was a candidate for the State Senate, but was defeated by the Hon. A. C. Downey. In 1868 he was a delegate to the National Convention, and under instructions of his constituency supported Pendleton until his name was withdrawn, and he had the satisfaction of having his course in that convention indorsed, upon his return, a satisfaction that some did not enjoy. As appears above, Mr. Pate has been a Democrat, and he is faithful still. Patrol is his postoffice address.

WILLIAM PATTERSON,

REPRESENTATIVE FROM SHELBY,

Was born in that county, February 11, 1827, and has resided there all the time since the day of his birth. His father was of Scotch descent, but, like his mother, of American birth. William never enjoyed the educational advantage that the average youth of the present day regards so irksome, but he did precisely what many boys of the present day fail to do. He availed himself of all the advantages for acquiring an education that could be had, and now he has more to show for it than many men who have attended school all their lives. He is now representative of the county of Shelby in the Indiana Legislature. This was a clear case of the office seeking the man, too. He had never before held an office and had no such aspirations. prefering the privacy of his farm in Jackson township.

In politics he is what he has been all his life, an

unflinching and a consistent Democrat. Mr. Patterson is a fit example for youth and manhood. He lives at Mt. Auburn.

NATHAN PEYEATT,

REPRESENTATIVE FROM WARRICK,

Is a native of Warren county, Kentucky, where he was born November 25, 1807. He descended from the French on one side, and from the Irish on the other. When ten years old he went to Illinois. He remembers distinctly to-day that the country was then a territory inhabited by wild beasts and Indians. He grew up with the country there until 1831. During his stay in the Sucker State he lived in the counties of Wayne, White, Edwards, Lawrence and Wabash. This was after the territorial government had given place to that of the State, and while the capital was at Vandalia. In 1831 he removed to Indiana, but in the following year he returned, married, and again repaired to Indiana and located on the farm in Warrick county, where he continues to date. From the densest woods he has fashioned a farm which it would excite the envy of an English lord to look upon. Mr. Peyeatt was educated in the common schools of the State of Illinois, and advanced to the rule of three in arithmetic, though he never saw a grammar in his school days. Such books were wholly unknown to the common schools of that day. He has reared a family of seven children, however, whom he has educated up to the times. Several of them are graduates, one of the State University, and he is now a practicing lawyer. Like all the other members of his father's family he lives in Warrick county. In politics Mr. Peyeatt has been a Democrat all his life. He cast his first Presidential vote for General Jackson, which should be a passport into any true Democratic caucus in the country. The gentleman from Warrick lives at Yankeetown.

SAMUEL RAMSEY,

REPRESENTATIVE FROM HARRISON,

Was born in Whitley county, Kentucky, January 24, 1830, of American parentage and Irish descent. With his parents he removed to Monroe county, in this State, when he was but one year old. There they remained until 1836, when they again removed, this time to near Fairdale, Harrison county, where the son still lives. He was trained to farm life, and continued to till the soil until he had reached manhood's estate; then he engaged in business as a merchant. Four years' experience in that business ended his mercantile pursuits, and he tried his hand at the mule and horse trade. That business he followed until he was thirty, when he began the study of law, which profession he practices now. He has hitherto held no office but that of Justice of the Peace three years, from 1855 to 1859. Politically he has been a life-long Democrat, steadfast in the faith, first, last and all the time. His legislative record is to make and to be written yet.

JOSEPH CLAYTON RATLIFF,

REPRESENTATIVE FROM WAYNE,

Is a native of that county, having been born there July 6, 1827. His parents were American. Joseph Clayton was educated at Richmond Academy, then took a course in the Western Reserve Medical College, in Cleveland, in 1851-2. For a time he practiced medicine and also dentistry. Then he returned to his farm and devoted himself to agricultural and horticultural pursuits. For six years he was President of the Wayne County Horticultural Society; for three years chief executive of the State Society. Three years he acted as President of the Wayne County Turnpike Company, and four years as Justice of the Peace.

He is known all over the State and the country as one who has done much to advance the agricultural and horticultural interests of Indiana.

Politically, he is Republican, but rather inclined to be liberal in his views, political and otherwise. His address is Richmond.

WILLIAM HENRY RAGAN,

REPRESENTATIVE FROM PUTNAM AND HENDRICKS,

Was born in Putnam county, this State. His parents were of Irish descent, but both were born in Virginia. The elder Ragan was one of the pioneers of Putnam county and of the State, having located near the present village of Fillmore, in 1823. Securing a tract of land, the senior Ragan began business as a nurseryman and fine fruit grower. Representative Ragan was educated partly in an old log school house near Fillmore, but mainly in the great school of nature—farming and horticulture. In 1860 he began the business of his father, for himself, on a part of the old homestead set apart for his culture. In 1865 he enlisted in the 11th Indiana infantry, then stationed at Baltimore City, and joining his regiment, he served therewith until the close of the war. In 1869 Mr. Ragan removed to Indianapolis, where he formed a co-partnership with J. C. Weinberger. in the management of the Bluff Road fruit farm, and there remained until 1871, when failing health admonished him that he had better return to rural life at the old home-stead, and be relieved of the arduous cares of the fruit farm, near this city. He has held quite a number of posi-tions of trust. In 1869 he served as Secretary of the Indi-ana Horticultural Society, and in 1873 was a member of the State Board of Agriculture. The same year he became editor of the Horticultural Department of the *Indiana Farmer*. In politics Mr. Ragan was a Democrat until 1861. when he became a Republican, and as such has acted since.

JACOB REDICK,

REPRESENTATIVE FROM RUSH,

Was born of Pennsylvania Dutch parentage. in Montgom-ery county. Ohio, April 14, 1811. His parents being poor, Jacob was apprenticed to a carpenter, and in the shop acquired his education. For fifteen years he pursued the phantom of prosperity with square and compass; then he turned his attention to farming. In his boyhood days, as he shoved the jackplane and wielded the saw he had not a thought of wielding so much influence as he does this winter over the destinies of his fellow men. He has been a resident of Indiana since 1832, and ought to have a pretty clearly-defined idea what his constituency and the State need in a legisative way.

MARTIN A. REEDER.

REPRESENTATIVE FROM RANDOLPH.

Was born in Warren county, Ohio, November 18th, 1819. His parents are reported as Pennsylvania Dutch and Massachusetts Yankee. The elder Reeder distinguished himself raising hair from the heads of the red skins in the times of Wayne and Harrison and under their commands. In 1822 the son, with his parents, removed to Indiana, where he was educated in a log school house, twenty feet square and seven feet high. This stupendous structure of primitive times, cost two or three days labor, and fifty cents in money, hard money of the blessed by-gone days of Democratic and Whig domination. The little debt was liquidated in one night, by the big boys who went coon hunting and secured the scalps of four coons. The pelts were disposed of to the Ewings of Fort Wayne, and the proceeds were applied to the payment of the debt incurred in erecting the said school house and the purchase of ammunition for a general Christmas deer hunt. In poli-t tics Mr. Reeder claims to have been a Jackson Democra until 1836, a Free Soiler Whig thence to 1856, acting as underground railroad conductor, then a Republican, and a Crusader and Anti-Monopolist. He says he is a decided advocate of the laboring classes, and in tossing up for choice of partners in a bear hunt would prefer an engineer to a railroad president, a section hand to a superintendent, and that he is decidedly opposed to giving a railroad President $40,000 per year and an everyday laborer on the road but $1 25 per day. He is an advocate of the equalization of salaries, and would vote in favor of paying school teachers more, State and county officers less. The gentleman from Randolph is evidently an anti-salary grabber. His postoffice address is Winchester

JESSE H. RENO,

REPRESENTATIVE FROM OWEN.

Is a native of Mercer county, Pennsylvania, where he was born in 1825. His parents were Americans. With them he removed to the West when he was quite young, and settled in Indiana. He managed to secure a substantial education in the common schools and through his own exertions at home. Nearly all his life he has been a resident of the sterling county he represents. During the last special and regular sessions of the Legislature he was a member of the House and served on several committees, and he is now Chairman of the Mileage Committee of that body. Politically he was always a Democrat of the positive kind Quincy is his address.

WILLIAM RIBBLE,

REPRESENTATIVE FROM DELAWARE,

Was born, of German parentage, in Montgomery county, Virginia, October 10, 1819. He came to this State in 1830, and settled near Selma, Delaware county, and has resided there on his farm ever since. He had none but a common school education. In 1844 he held the office of Justice of the Peace; was a Whig then, but is a Republican now. His life heretofore has been the uneventful one of a farmer—"at peace with all the world, and the rest of mankind." In the year 1835-'36 his father represented Delaware county in the State Legislature. Having followed the avocation of his father in private life it seems that he is destined also to follow in his footsteps in public life. Those who would like to know what he knows about farming can address the gentleman from Delaware at Selma.

JAMES ROMINE,

REPRESENTATIVE FROM SPENCER,

Was born in the county of Spencer, March 12, 1832. His father was from Missouri and his mother from Kentucky. They removed to Indiana as early as 1816, and settled in Spencer. They were among the very first settlers in Spencer county. The elder Romine held, in his time, about all the offices made and provided for in that county. The son was educated in the common schools of his native neighborhood, and has a very fair English education to show for it. Farming has been his occupation all his life, and he has followed it faithfully with the exception of four or five years, a decade ago, when he filled the office of Recorder of Spencer county. He must be a very popular personage, for his county has been Republican for years. and, though he had always been a Democrat, he was elected to the Legislature last fall by 541 votes, running ahead of the State ticket throughout the county. Even a Democrat who could keep up with the ticket at the last election is no sluggard in a race, to say nothing of running ahead of it, as Mr. Romine did. Gentryville is his postoffice address.

WILLIAM NEWTON ROSEBERRY,

REPRESENTATIVE FROM MONROE,

Was born in Bourbon county. Kentucky, October 8, 1814. His father and mother were born at Cane Ridge, Bourbon county, Ky., and of American parentage. Nathaniel Rogers, one of the members of the old Constitutional Convention of Kentucky, and the last who died, was a grandfather of the gentleman whose name appears above. William Newton only enjoyed such educational facilities as the common schools of Kentucky and Indiana, in pioneer times, could give. He came to this State with his parents and settled in Monroe county in 1827, and there he still lives. He was a tiller of the soil until 1840, when he was elected Justice of the Peace, and served until 1855. Since then he has been speculating in mules. Politically, Mr. Roseberry is a Democrat of the square-toed stamp. His post office address is Rosecreek.

A. H. SHAFFER, M. D.,

REPRESENTATIVE FROM WABASH AND HUNTINGTON,

Was born in Starke county, State of Ohio, January 15, 1829. His parents were of American birth, but of German extraction. He was educated in the University of Michigan and Western Reserve Medical College, of Ohio. In 1856 he came to this State and located at Huntington, and commenced the practice of his profession. Entering the army early in the war, he was assigned to duty as assistant surgeon, and was subsequently promoted to the position of surgeon of the 75th Ohio, and served therein until the close of the war. Since then he has practiced his profession at Huntington, as before. He is Republican in politics and expects so to remain. His home is at Huntington.

JOHN NEWTON SHAW,

REPRESENTATIVE FROM DECATUR.

Was born in Campbell county, Kentucky, January 29, 1817. On his father's side his ancestors were of Irish descent, but Welsh on the side of his mother. Both parents were born in America, and their fathers were soldiers in the Revolutionary War. They were known to fame as James Shaw and Edward Moran. Mr. Shaw's father and mother removed to Kentucky from Pennsylvania and Virginia, respectively, in the olden times. From thence they removed to Missouri, and thence came the subject of this sketch to Decatur county in 1844, where he has continued to reside since then. Heretofore he has been a far-

mer, serving some sixteen years as Justice of the Peace
when resting from rural pursuits. 'Squire Shaw is known
throughout Decatur county as one of the most substantial
citizens of the county, and a life-long Democrat.

SAMUEL SHORTRIDGE,

REPRESENTATIVE FROM TIPPECANOE,

Is a native of that county, for which he has the honor to
speak in the Legislative session of 1874–'75. He was born
in 1830, August 4, which places him at this writing in the
forty-fifth year of his age. Mr. Shortridge comes of one
of the substantial families of Indiana farmers. His father
was one of the early Sheriffs of Tippecanoe county, in
which office he served altogether eight years and represented his county in the General Assembly two terms.
The present incumbent has acted as Trustee of his township eleven years in succession. He is first cousin of
President A. C. Shortridge, of the Purdue University, and
himself a farmer of means and progressive habit. As
may be presumed, the foundation of his education was laid
in the public school, which is honored and vindicated by
its graduates in the highest council of the commonwealth.
The paternal branch of the family is English, and the
maternal side leads back to both Irish and German blood.
In Mr. Shortridge as a law-maker the people are certain
of an honest and trustworthy friend, who will use all the
influence he possesses to promote the best good of society
and the prosperity of his native State, to whose public
service he has been called. Lafayette is his address.

CORNELIUS SHUGART,

REPRESENTATIVE FROM GRANT,

Was born in Wayne county, Indiana, February 9, 1820. His parents were of American birth and English extraction. The son was educated at Richmond, where he passed the first fourteen years of his life. Then he removed to Grant county, where he has lived for forty years, and has had the happiness of seeing that portion of the State become, from a howling wilderness, great and populous. For the first few years of his life in the county, Mr. Shugart was a teacher ; since, a farmer. He claims to be "but a small man of limited ability," yet a full believer in the adage, " Duty is ours ; consequences belong to God ;" and also a strenuous advocate, as well as believer in, temperance in all things.

He has heretofore held no office but that of Supervisor of a very muddy road, to which position of trust he was unanimously elected. Politically speaking, he is a Republican ; but strictly, not a strenuous politician. Jonesboro is the address of the gentleman from Grant.

MATTHEW ALEXANDER SMITH,

JOINT REPRESENTATIVE FROM JAY AND DELAWARE,

Was born in Brunswick county, Virginia, March 28, 1819. His parents were of English extraction. His education was received in the common schools of Greene county, Ohio, and he removed to Indiana in 1840. He had been in this State but two years before he was elected Justice of the Peace, and he served fourteen years. Then he was elected County

10

Commissioner, and so served until 1862. In 1865 he was elected again, and served until 1871. When not engaged exclusively in the discharge of official duties he has been engaged in farming. Politically he was a Whig until 1856, then a Republican, and a Republican still. He has always been an advocate of temperance, and at the same time has been strictly temperate. His address is Albany, Delaware county.

DESIGNEY ALBERT SNYDER,

REPRESENTATIVE FROM MARSHALL,

Was born in Marshall county, Indiana, November 17, 1847. His father was a farmer of the old Virginia school, and trained his son in the way he had been taught to earn a livelihood. The son's educational opportunities in boyhood were confined to the common schools of the State. But he demonstrated the fact that the system of common schools in Indiana is capable of giving a good education to those who will apply themselves assiduously they having brains to begin with. Learning the law several years since, and proceeding to practice his profession, Mr. Snyder succeeded so well that he has been called upon by the Democrats of his native county to represent them in the Legislature. The gentleman from Marshall is a young man of ability and ably represents one of the best counties in the State.

HARVEY TAYLOR,

REPRESENTATIVE FROM DAVIESS,

Was born in Rockcastle county, Kentucky, April 10, 1821. His parents were of American birth, and natives of Virginia. He took a course in the common schools of Kentucky, and at the age of twenty he left his native State, and emigrated to Indiana. Once in the State, he worked about from farm to farm for four or five years, when he commenced the study of medicine with Dr. John Hill, of Monroe county, and after reading there one year, he left and located in Lawrence county, where he entered the office of Dr. Free, and continued to prosecute his professional studies. In 1849 he removed to Daviess county, and resumed practice. There he has lived and flourished ever since, a living monument of the self-made men indigenous to Western soil. He is now a bright and shining light of the Daviess County Medical Society, and the Indiana Legislature.

Dr. Taylor has served the State on the field of battle too, and when life's fitful fever is over, his posterity can point with pride to the record he made there as well as in the halls of State. His military career was inaugurated by his enlistment in and elevation to the Second Lieutenantcy of a company in the 14th Indiana. In 1863 he entered the 65th regiment, where he ascended the scale of commissioned promotion to the third degree, retiring to his rural home in 1865, covered all over with glory, and a brace of bars on either shoulder.

The only office he ever held in civil life, before the one he now holds, was Township Assessor, in 1855 to 1856.

Politically, he was a Whig, so long as the organization

was perpetuate, then a Republican until his honesty and self respect rebelled against its corruption, since when he has been a Democrat.   He resides near Rugglesville.

SAMUEL M. TAYLOR,

JOINT REPRESENTATIVE FROM HAMILTON AND TIPTON,

Is a native of Wayne county, Indiana, where he was born April 19, 1829.   He can trace his lineage back to England, Germany and the Emerald Isle, but don't care to go back beyond his native State, being well satisfied with it.   He was educated in the common schools and at the academies of Muncie and Newcastle.   At the conclusion of his academic course, he read law with Messrs. Elliott & Mellett, but never engaged in the practice of his profession, preferring mercantile life to the traditional nine years of starvation preceding the remunerative practice of law.   During the war he served in the 101st Regiment Indiana Volunteers. Again engaging in active mercantile pursuits, with the added occupation of trading, at the close of the war, he has been so engaged since.   He has held about all the offices within the gift of the people of his adopted village, but the county was too Democratic for a Republican to become Clerk, as he learned upon second trial.   But he is a Republican still, having kept the faith.   He lives at Tipton.

DANIEL THOMAS,

REPRESENTATIVE FROM PARKE.

Was born at Saratoga Springs, New York State, February 15, 1814. His parents were Welsh and German. With his father's family he removed to Indiana in 1825. When he had attained his majority he removed to Parke county, where he has resided thirty-eight years. He was educated in the common schools of the State and has followed farming all his life, having held none but township offices. In politics he was a Jackson Democrat during the last term of old Hickory. But he was an anti-Van Buren man, and he swears that the social relations of old Dick Johnson were too dark for him to follow in his footsteps, politically speaking. He is a Republican now, having been trained to follow in the dark and dubious party paths. Portland Mills, Parke county, is his address.

ADDISON R. A. THOMPSON,

JOINT REPRESENTATIVE FROM HENRY AND MADISON,

Was born in Muskingum county, Ohio, March 29th, 1818. His parents were natives of Virginia. In 1836, Addison first set foot upon the soil of this, his adopted State. He took his first lessons in the alphabet under the tutelage of John Purdue, now of Lafayette. In 1838, while making his home at Covington, he traveled one thousand miles on horseback, visiting Iowa, then a vast wilderness. Notwithstanding this remarkable equestrian feat of his earlier manhood, Mr. Thompson would hesitate before attempting to ride two horses running in opposite

directions around the political arena. In fact he did hesitate and picking out the Independent horse he abandoned
to the crows the spavined and otherwise "stove up"
Republican horse which he had before ridden. Thus
he rode slowly but surely into the public crib. But
this is digression. In the spring of 1840, Mr. Thompson
embarked in a flat boat at Covington, and made a trip to
the Crescent city. At Nachez, he cast anchor for a few
days, to view the wreck wrought in the city by the whirl-
wind that year. It was something like the tidal wave of
last fall, in violence.

During the existence of that organization, Mr. Thompson was a Whig, then a Republican, now an Independent.
He never held any office other than the one to which he
was lately elected. Blountsville is his address.

JAMES LEE THOMPSON,

REPRESENTATIVE FROM MARION,

Was born in Hamilton county, Ohio, in 1818. His parents
were both American, and his father represented Fayette
county in the Legislature two years, having removed to
Indiana with his family in 1833. The son was reared
upon his father's farm in Fayette, and afterwards followed
farming for a livelihood. All the education he ever
received was secured in the common schools of the county,
such as they were at that early day. Since beginning
life for himself he has lived in Rush, Clinton and Howard
counties, but is now located for life, most likely, near
Acton, in Marion county. In his time he has held office

eight years—before the present. In politics he is a staunch Democrat, one not ashamed to stand up before the world and avow the principles of his party through good and through evil report.

MILTON TRUSLER,

JOINT REPRESENTATIVE FROM FAYETTE AND UNION,

Was born in Franklin county, Indiana, August 31, 1825. His parents were from Virginia and removed to Indiana in 1812. He was educated in the common schools, and engaged in agriculture, as he had been trained on his father's farm. He followed that uneventful avocation until the spring of 1861, when he was elected Trustee for Jackson township, and continued to hold the office through repeated partiality on the part of the people until last August, when he resigned and was elected to the Legislature soon afterwards. When the Whig party was in existence he professed the principles of that faith, and acted with that party. Upon the organization of the Republican party he joined that, and he is now, as he has been since then, a Republican, and was elected as such to the office he now holds. His home is Everton.

WILLIAM TWIBILL,

JOINT REPRESENTATIVE FROM GRANT AND BLACKFORD,

Was born in Whitsit county, Virginia, October 29, 1831. His parents were of American birth. They left old Virginia and removed to Indiana in 1834, and settled in Blackford county. There the son was educated in the common schools and settled down near the old homestead to the slow but honest occupation of an agriculturist. In 1856 he tired of the toil of farm life, and engaged in the dry goods trade, in which business he remained until the war, when he enlisted in the 34th Indiana Infantry and was commissioned Captain of Company "I," over which he exercised such command until mustered out of the service. When he had returned from the war he engaged in the hardware business, meantime speculating in stock, grain, produce, and anything in which there was any money. In politics he has been a Republican from the beginning, and will continue faithful to the end if the party is true to itself. Montpelier is the postoffice address of the gentleman from Blackford and Grant.

JOHN WALTZ,

REPRESENTATIVE FROM POSEY,

Was born at Aberwistadt, in the Grand Duchy of Baden, February 28, 1829. Mr. Waltz was educated in the Polytechnic School at Menheim, Baden. After having taken part in the revolution of 1848 in the old country, he left it for free America, landing in New York City in March, 1851. Leaving the metropolis in the fall, and setting out for the West, he stopped off at Cincinnati, but hearing there of Indiana, he of course left for the promised land at once, and located at Evansville. Subsequently he settled down at New Harmony, in Posey county; but he didn't go into the hoop-pole business, as might be charged if the writer were not more explicit. He began business there as a boot and shoe manufacturer, and is yet so engaged. During his stay in the capital in the service of the State, his business is in charge of a trusty foreman. He is one of the tried and true citizens of the community in which he lives. He is now Treasurer of the Workingmens' Institute; Treasurer of New Harmony Lodge, I. O. O. F.; has been three or four times Trustee of Posey County Agricultural Association, and is at present; and he has held other positions of trust, if not profit. Since his advent into this country he has been a Democrat. The first vote he ever cast for President was for Franklin Pierce, and the last, for Horace Greeley. Hitherto he has not held any position through political preferment. For the office he now holds he was nominated without his knowledge and consent. He is a widower, and his post-office address is New Harmony.

THOMAS WASHBURN,

REPRESENTATIVE FROM WHITLEY,

Was born in Harrison county, West Virginia, July 28, 1805. His family before him had descended from the Welsh. In 1843 he came to this State and settled in Whitley county, having first spent several years in the State of Ohio, before he had heard of the promised land, and in Whitley he has abided ever since. By occupation he is a carpenter, surveyor and merchant. In Ohio and Indiana he held the office of Justice of the Peace, and discharged the duties of the office with the dignity becoming that exalted office. He was Auditor of Whitley county four years from 1844, and State Senator in 1852. He is Democratic first, last and all the time. Mr. Washburn resides near Columbia City.

MILES WATERMAN,

Was born in the town of Camillus, Onondaga county, N. Y., December 22, 1818. His father was a descendant from Plymouth Rock and his mother, like his father, from Massachusetts, but of Irish extraction. In 1837, Miles, like the star of empire, Westward wended his way, having first received a common school education, however. He had heard of Indiana, and of course came here direct, locating in DeKalb county. Immediately upon his arrival, he adopted the vocation of farming. In 1846 he was taken from the plow and put into the Auditor's Office of his adopted county, and he did so well that he was kept there until 1855. In 1858–9 he was a member of the House, Indiana Legislature, representing DeKalb county. This was a special session. In 1863 he was elected a member of the House and served in the regular session. Besides, he has represented his county in many minor offices.

Politically Mr. Waterman was, until of late years, a Democrat of Douglas and Lecompton principles. He is now a Granger. In the canvass for the Legislature in 1862, for the session of 1862, the war then being in progress, he took the position that the government was legally in the hands of the Republican party, and that the war for the suppression of the rebellion should be energetically prosecuted, but did not believe the leaders of that party were honestly prosecuting the war for the suppression of the rebellion and the restoration of the union simply, there then being too many union-sliders among them. On the financial question he claims to be, nominally, a hard-money man, maintaining that when the currency has been inflated it should be reduced very gradually. He also entertains the opinion that the too sudden contraction of the currency since the war has been the main cause of our financial troubles. He contends that contraction at the North has been much greater than most people seem to suppose, the drain to supply the South having caused a large share of this contraction. He thinks an increase of a few millions at this time would be beneficial. Then, he believes that greenbacks should be the currency of the country; else, banking should be free. Mr. Waterman is a resident of Waterloo.

OLIVER D. WILLETT,

REPRESENTATIVE FROM NOBLE,

Was born in Richland county, Ohio, March 23d, 1835. His parents were natives of Maryland, of English descent. When he was only sixteen years of age Mr. Willett left the paternal roof and courted fickle fortune in Williams county, Ohio. He remained there until 1870, when he moved to Noble county, this State. He has been prosperous in business from the beginning and is now managing head of the extensive marble manufactories of O. D. Willett & Co., Noblesville. Mr. Willett is a gentleman of fine presence and admirable social qualities. Politically he is a Democrat and has been all his life.

ALFRED WILLIAMS,

Was born in Overton county, East Tennessee, November 6, 1822. His parents were of American birth. His grandfather, John J. Williams, was a soldier of the Revolution, and was twice or thrice taken prisoner by the minions of King George III. His name was on the pension rolls until the date of his death in 1849, at the advanced age of 95 years. He was a native of the State of North Carolina, but died in Georgia His son was a native of Surrey county, North Carolina, and served in the war of 1812, as Second Lieutenant in a Federal regiment, participating in the battle of New Orleans, June 8, 1815. In 1825 Mr. Williams removed to this State and settled, where the surviving members of the family now reside. He was the first Treasurer appointed for Brown county, before a permanent organization was perfected, and also the first one elected by the people of the county after its organization.

Alfred, himself, had but poor opportunities for securing an education, yet he has all the book learning necessary, as well as the experience of an active business life. He became a practical surveyor through his own teaching, from such text books as he could secure. In 1854 he had so thoroughly mastered the science of surveying that he was made Assistant Surveyor of Brown county, and as is the case with assistants generally, he had to perform the duties of the office. In 1856 he was elected Surveyor and re-elected in 1858. In 1862 he was elected County Treasurer, served two years, and was again elected. In 1866 he was elected Representative to the Lower House of the Legislature from Brown county, and at the last election, as appears above, Joint Representative from Brown and Bartholomew. He is, and always has been, a Democrat of the conservative character. For " recollections of a busy life." address Mr. Williams, at Nashville, Indiana.

ANDREW JACKSON WILLIAMS,

REPRESENTATIVE FROM LAWRENCE,

Was born in Blount county, East Tennessee. June 5, 1815. He was only two years old when. with his parents, he came to Indiana and located in Lawrence county. The county was new at that time, and it is indelibly impressed upon the tablets of his memory that potatoes were mighty scarce that season. They arrived there in the fall, and he avers that he can remember how his mother cried, during the winter that ensued, because they had no potatoes. Late in the summer following that winter, however, his mother was made happy by the mature growth of a bountiful crop. For the period of a year preceding they had to subsist on venison and bear meat and hogs, which they then hunted like bear. Those were regarded as hard times, but Mr. Williams still lives. Though he never married he had the responsibility of rearing twenty-two children. It came about in this way : Many of his near relatives died at different times during the last quarter of a century, and he assumed the care and culture of their children, clothing and educating them. As a raiser of crops and stock, he has been equally successful. His farm, near Fayetteville, is one of the finest in the State. But he has not been a farmer all his life, having taught school for a few years when a " peart young man." Politically the gentleman from Lawrence was a Democrat until the repeal of the Missouri compromise, since when he has been a Republican.

SAMUEL WOODY,

JOINT REPRESENTATIVE FROM HOWARD AND MIAMI,

Is a native of North Carolina, having been born in Orange county in that State, April 14th, 1828. With his parents he removed to Indiana and settled near Bloomingdale, in Parke county, in 1829, and was educated in the common schools of that county. His father lost all in the financial panic, which debarred the realization of the expectation of the son's boyhood days, a collegiate education. With his aged parents and an afflicted sister, he settled where he now lives, in the then wilderness of the Miami Reservation, and there he has hewn from the forest, his fine farm of three hundred acres. In politics he was formerly a Whig but is a Republican now, and has been since the organization of that party. Of offices he has held those of Township Trustee and Representative. Four years ago he was a candidate for the State Senate, but was defeated by the Hon. A. F. Armstrong on the reform cry of the cunning candidate. Last election he was nominated for joint representative from Miami and Howard, and having had some experience as a candidate he "whipped the fight" and won the race. He has been through the mill and is now competent to imitate the aspiring young politician. His address is Russiaville, Miami county.

JAMES MARCELLUS WYNN,

REPRESENTATIVE FROM JENNINGS,

Was born in Franklin county, Indiana, February 19, 1833. His parents were both English. The elder Wynn came to this country and settled at Brookville when but eighteen years of age (this was in 1818). He was friendless and alone, and had but one single shilling at his command. Having a good, general, and a first class mathematical education, he secured the situation of teacher for a season and subsequently that of surveyor of Franklin county. He received his remuneration for teaching in the consideration of the county, such as oats and other products of the soil. He was elected surveyor several times ; was then chosen Cashier of the Brookville Bank, and Secretary of a prominent local railroad, besides many other positions of trust and profit. He died in Jennings county in 1861, leaving a large family and an ample fortune for their maintenance.

James Marcellus, the one of these children made the subject of this sketch, moved from the house where he was born to the one in which he now lives. He has been a farmer all his life, though he acquired a very fine education in his early days. For two years he was County Surveyor. In 1872 he was elected to represent Jennings county in the Lower House, and last fall re-elected, running ahead of his ticket. He claims to be a black Republican, a temperance man, by example as well as precept—having never tasted whisky—and a Methodist. When young, his wife thought him a handsome man. Scipio is his postoffice address.

www.ingramcontent.com/pod-product-compliance
Lightning Source LLC
Chambersburg PA
CBHW021114020726

47500CB00003B/760